I Remember

12/2011

Hibah dear,

This is for you to remember me once in a while if not always... sending my heart and appreciation of your friendship and love to you...

Love,
Rowena :)

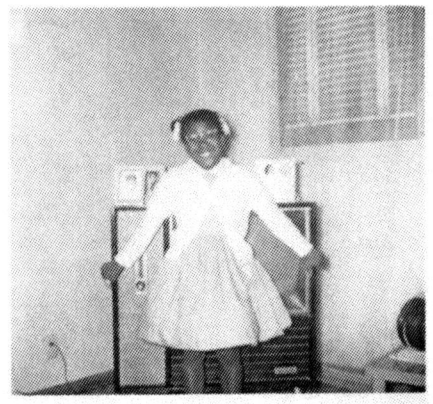

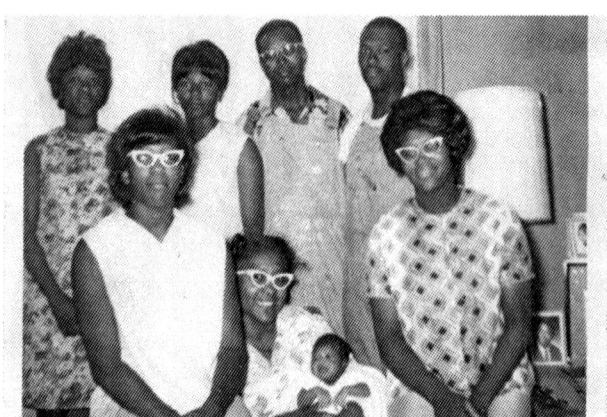

I Remember

A Collection of Short Stories from My Childhood

Vetress A. Arnold

Writer's Showcase
presented by *Writer's Digest*
San Jose New York Lincoln Shanghai

I Remember
A Collection of Short Stories from My Childhood

All Rights Reserved © 2000 by Vetress A. Arnold

No part of this book may be reproduced or transmitted in any form or by any means, graphic, electronic, or mechanical, including photocopying, recording, taping, or by any information storage retrieval system, without the permission in writing from the publisher.

Writer's Showcase
presented by *Writer's Digest*
an imprint of iUniverse.com, Inc.

For information address:
iUniverse.com, Inc.
620 North 48th Street, Suite 201
Lincoln, NE 68504-3467
www.iuniverse.com

"Playing in the Basement" was previously published in
Turtle Cove Creative Magazine.
Jacket photograph by Vetress A. Arnold
Author photograph © Carousel Portraiture

ISBN: 0-595-12566-2

Printed in the United States of America

To Moma. I love you, I miss you, and I will always pray for your soul.

Contents

Acknowledgements ix
Introduction xi
A Night Alone 1
I'm Gonna Tell 4
Taking a Nap 7
Our New Car 10
Making Mud Pies 12
Ants 14
Grandmother 16
The First Grade 19
Tip, Spot, Dick, and Jane 22
The Uncle Jimmy Show 24
Wearing Glasses 27
Going to Church 29
Bible Study 32
Nick Names 34
Celebrities 37

Asthma Attacks 39
Get the Soap 41
Abuse 43
Playing in the Basement 46
Piano Lessons 49
The Blacks 52
The Mills 55
Miss Alice 58
My Sister's Boyfriend 60
Kemper's 62
Conversations with the Devil 64
Boley 66
A Heavenly Dream 69
The Holiness Church 72
Mr. Thinn 75
My First Period 78
The Responsible One 80
Conclusion 83
About the Author 85

ACKNOWLEDGEMENTS

All praise is due to the Heavenly Father.

I'd like to thank Paulette Alexander, who gracefully accepted the tedious job of proofreading my draft.

I'd like to thank my family and friends, who continually showed their love, support, and encouragement.

I'd like to thank all of you, who thought I'd never make it. You made me try harder.

INTRODUCTION

Many people remember some of their childhood. Some people remember much of their childhood. I remember most of my childhood. I don't know why or what purpose it serves, but I do. Certain people are amazed by my memory, while others just think, "so what."

Family has been, is now, and always will be, very important to me. Moma played an integral part in my development. I credit her with my sensitivity, awareness, honesty, and compassion. She taught me that no matter what, you should always believe in God and do what's right. And, I have tried to live up to that expectation.

I have wonderful friends whom I consider as much a part of my family as anyone. They have been extremely supportive and encouraging, even when I doubted myself. They have helped me to realize that giving up on your dreams is one of the greatest sins you can commit against yourself.

This collection of short stories represents my true recollection of growing up in Yakima, Washington. They consist of memories from infancy through about age 13. However, keep in mind that these memories are seen through the eyes of a young, immature observer (that would be me!). I have tried, with the best of my ability, to write each incident as accurately as possible. Of course, facts as seen from a child's perspective may be different than those remembered from an older sibling (that would be my sisters!). Regardless, these are my feelings as *I* remember them.

So what about my later years in life? Those memories I've reserved for the next volume(s). Stay tuned…

I feel blessed to have the opportunity and ability to share these stories with you. I hope you can relate to them, and more importantly, enjoy them.

A Night Alone

I remember being in a rather large crib; however, I can't quite remember how old I was. The crib had light blue plastic bars (to keep me from getting out, I suspect) and a blue-and-white patterned crib mattress. I think the pattern was little babies. They were all laughing and holding rattles. I often wondered just what was so funny to them. Being the last of five children, I'm sure it was a very used crib. It was in my parent's bedroom. Yes, back then they did sleep together, on most nights anyway. That is until I was old enough to take over their bed. At that point, my father decided to sleep in the basement, which was a good decision. More room for me and Moma!

I was told, later on in life, that I was a mistake. Moma should have never had any more kids. Was that my problem? Well…

One night my mother and father actually went out on the town with another couple. I'm guessing they went out on the town. All I know is that they went someplace, and they were all dressed up. And I wasn't going! My mother was very attractive and my father was dapper as usual. I was told to be a good girl and that my sisters would take care of me. Moma kissed me on her way out. I was happy and snug as a bug in a rug.

Then it happened. I awakened after a brief nap and found the room to be pitch black. I couldn't see a thing. I could hear no noise, see nothing, and I felt as though I must have been the only person left on the face of the earth. Where was everybody? Surely, if I cried someone would come and rescue me. That always worked. I started off with a small whimper because that usually did the trick. It also meant I wouldn't have to exert too much energy to get the job done (that energy would need to be saved for other activities, such as eating). To my surprise no one responded. I thought to myself, "how could this be?" It always worked in the past. Maybe I wasn't loud enough. I had to consider that my sisters were in the other bedroom way on the other side of the house (it seemed like such a big house back then). It wasn't like my mother was right next to me and could hear whether my breathing had missed a beat. She always responded immediately. She was such a good mother! She knew what mattered in life. She knew how important I was.

Okay, I thought. I'll let out a short cry, but boy they'd better come running quickly. I was, after all, the baby and I needed attention! Again, no response. Now I'm worried. How could they not come running? Something might have actually been wrong with me. Were they crazy? Did they not hear Moma's instruction that I was to be taken care of? Did they not understand the seriousness of the situation at hand? Did they not know whom they were dealing with? I was the baby. I was so cute with black curly hair and big brown eyes. I ruled that house. Whatever I wanted, I got. How dare they not come to my rescue immediately! I'd show them. I'd cry for real, and they'd be sorry (probably the neighbors, too).

I cried for what seemed to be an eternity. First I cried softly. Then I pumped up the volume. I went from making short screams to producing long wailing sounds. I jumped up and down in my crib and staged a full-blown tantrum. I used the rattle to rake the bars on the crib (like prisoners with their tin cups) and kicked and screamed until I choked. I screamed and screamed and screamed. My lungs were burning, my cheeks were hurting, my chubby legs were giving way, and my knuckles were turning red from squeezing the crib bars so tight. The tears were endless. I was all wet. My little, round, button nose was running like Niagara Falls. I felt like a prisoner. After all, didn't they at least get bread and water? This was inhumane treatment. Why were they doing this to me? I was a little angel. Is this how little angels were treated? My protest fell on deaf ears. Nobody came for me. What was I to do? Was anyone home? Was I left all alone? Was I going to die? But, I had only lived a short time. It wasn't fair. Everyone else got to live a long time. They were old. Why me? Was it because Moma wasn't supposed to have any more kids? That wasn't my fault. How could it be? I shouldn't be blamed. Yet, I was the one made to suffer—the littlest, the cutest, the most important. I was doomed.

I don't know how long this went on. It felt like days. Surely, I was dead. All I know is, I woke up to the soothing sounds of Moma saying, "My poor baby was so upset, she had to mess in her pants." Is that why I was so wet? I thought it was the tears. Hey, I was okay after all. The lights were on again, and Moma was holding me. Brother, what an ordeal! Those dirty-dog sisters of mine. Where were they anyway? If only I could talk, I'd get them in big trouble. Just wait, I'd tell...

I'm Gonna Tell

I remember my older sisters were always doing something they had no business doing. Moma told them not to do it, but they did it anyway. They knew they were going to get in trouble. They knew they were going to get whuppings. I just couldn't understand them. They were the oldest. Weren't they supposed to be the smartest?

I used to beg them, "Please don't do it. You know you're going to get in trouble. Moma said don't do it. You know what Moma said." But you know what they said to me? They said, "Oh shut up." I told them I was gonna tell. I told them they were going to get in trouble.

They used to give me money not to tell. Sometimes, I would get nickels. If they were doing something really bad, I'd get quarters. In addition to getting the money, cuz' "show me the money" was my motto, I got to watch. I always wanted to see what they were doing. I wanted to see, first hand, what was worth getting a whupping over. Were they going to go outside the yard? We weren't supposed to go outside the yard for any reason if Moma wasn't home. That offense would be worth a nickel. Were they going to have those boys over and play in the garage? This really interested me. Those boys were no good, and my sisters knew it. I don't know why my sisters liked them. They weren't even cute. That offense would be worth a quarter (and sometimes more depending on what they were doing in the garage).

All I know is nothing, I mean nothing, was worth one of those whuppings Moma could give. She'd whup you 'til her arms got tired. It seemed like her arms NEVER got tired. And if they did, she would rest until they weren't tired anymore and then she would whup you some more! She used to whup you with belts, coat hangers, ironing cords, or whatever was handy. One time, she took one of my sisters to the basement to give the whupping. If you got whupped in the basement, God help you. She would whup them so hard their backs would be bleeding. Then she would put salt on their backs. They would howl like coyotes in heat during a full moon. It would scare me to death. But, I couldn't do a thing to save them. All I could say was, "I told them not to do it. I told them they were going to get in trouble. I told them I was gonna tell."

Now, I wasn't stupid. I got the money first, then I'd tell. I would say innocently, "Moma, you know what they did today? I tried to tell them, Moma. I tried to tell them not to do it. I told them you said not to, but they did it anyway, Moma." You have to understand, it's not like I wanted them to get a whupping (that was a terrifying experience). But, at the same time, I felt this compelling need to tell. It was the right thing to do. After all, I was the baby, and the baby had to do the right thing. Were they ever going to learn?

We weren't allowed to go a lot of places. We had to go to church and always do our homework. We were the respectable Arnold girls. But one of the places we were allowed to frequent was the park. We would go to the park everyday. The park was cool, and everybody went to the park. Sometimes it would seem like the whole town was there, especially on Sundays. And we knew them all. There was a swimming pool, swings (a set for the big kids and a separate set for the little kids), a sandbox, a merry-go-round, a slide, and picnic tables.

Every Sunday after church, all of the older men would sit under this certain tree and play dominoes all day long. They would slap those wooden picnic tables real hard with their "bones" (dominoes which were made of ivory and thus I assumed meant "tusks" or animal teeth/bones) and would call each other "Spody." I often wondered just who this "Spody" person was. Recently, I asked my father about this. I asked him if "Spody" was slang for "Sporty." At first, he just looked at me rather puzzled. Then, I provided a lengthy explanation of what I meant and why I wanted to know. I gave him my thoughts on the subject and asked him to confirm my accurateness. After asking me how to spell it, he went on to tell me that "Sporty" was used to describe a person with good sportsman-like qualities. This person had to be good at whatever game he was playing. Ah, sweet mysteries of life!

There was also a junior high school (Washington Junior High School) right across the street that had a baseball field and a gym where people could play basketball.

My sisters used to meet their no-good boyfriends at the park. Now they knew they weren't supposed to be talking to these boys, not at the park or anywhere else. But they figured since the park was so big, if Moma was to come driving around to see what they were doing, they would see her first. That would give them time to stop talking to those no-good boys. No harm, no foul. Well…you had to get up pretty early to fool Moma. Somehow she always managed to catch them. They would get busted, right at the park, and in front of everyone. How embarrassing! Moma would make them get in the car, and she would whup them while she was driving! I'd be in the front seat, of course. The front seat was the best seat in the house. Fitting for the baby, don't you think?

Sitting in the front seat made me feel like I was kinda in charge. You have to admit that position does have some kind of authority associated with it. Maybe that's why little kids always fight over who's going to sit in front. And you know that old compromise: you sit in front on the way up, and somebody else sits in front on the way back. Unless, of course, they're getting a whupping.

Taking a Nap

I remember when I had to take naps during the day. It wasn't like I got banished to my room with the door shut. I got to lay down on the couch in the living room. No matter, it was still torture. Moma would be in her bedroom trying to catch a few minutes of rest. I knew better than to make any noise. That would mean big trouble.

If I turned around just right, I could see Moma lying in her bed sleeping. I had to look through the dining room and between some chairs. She always kept her bedroom door open and would be in plain view. I often wondered how she could possibly like taking naps. It was dull and boring. I would wish for the telephone to ring. Moma would have to get out of her bed and run into the kitchen to answer it. Perhaps, I thought, after all of that activity she would concede and let me get up. That rarely happened.

I would lie on that couch and sing songs to myself. Most of the songs I made up. They were really silly, but it kept me amused. I used to kick the blanket off me and then try to put it back on with my feet. It was no fair touching it with your hands. I would pretend I was a princess living in a palace. There were so many servants around that I never had to do anything. I would wonder what I would have for lunch. Maybe today we would have tomato soup and crackers or tuna fish sandwiches. Then I would hum the Campbell's soup song. You know the one: ummmm good, that's what Campbell's soup is, ummmm good. I would wonder when my sisters were coming home from school. It was so quiet in the house. I could hear the birds singing outside. I would wonder if they made up the songs they were singing too. But how would the other birds know what song to sing? They all seemed to be in tune with each other. This was a mystery that was never solved.

I could hear the hum of the refrigerator in the kitchen. Then I would think about how my sister and I used to scrape the ice that formed in the freezer section with a butter knife and eat it. It was like eating a snow cone, but without the colored flavoring. We weren't supposed to do that cuz' it would ruin the refrigerator or make us sick. But we used to sneak and do it anyway. One of us would be the lookout while the other scraped. We were a good team. She didn't play with me often, but when she did, we had a good time. Later on she told me that somebody told her eating that ice would keep you from getting pregnant. Well, she had two kids…

I would think about how my oldest sister would let me eat flour from the flour bin. It would stick to the roof of my mouth, and I couldn't talk. It was sorta like eating peanut butter. My oldest sister could cook good. She used to make cakes and let me lick the spoon. I loved eating the batter as much as the frosting. Of course, I got to lick the bowl, too. I would beg her to leave extra in the bowl for me to eat. She always did. I think she liked me best. After all, I was the baby. Whenever she made homemade biscuits, I would get to cut some out using a Ball canning jar or a plastic Tupperware cup. I would do it ever so carefully so they would be just perfect. When she made yeast bread, she would put butter, brown sugar, and cinnamon in some so they were really sweet.

I would think about how my sister used to go downstairs, look through my father's pockets and find money. I used to wonder how she knew where to look cuz' she always found it. Sometimes she would buy me an ice cream from the ice cream man. I always liked to get popsicles cuz' you could break them apart and pretend you had two. The multi-flavored one (orange, yellow, and red) was the best. After we were done we'd make lattice fences with the used popsicle sticks. You had to make sure you licked them clean; otherwise, the fences would be all sticky, and the ants would try to seize them as their home.

I would think about putting away the groceries after going to the grocery store. All of the canned goods went on the shelves in the basement. My sister and I used to pretend we were checkers at the checkout stand. She would hand me the canned goods, and I would put them on the shelf. I would make the cash register noise as I did it, cha-ching!

After all of this thinking I would be tired and fall asleep. Moma used to tell me what a good girl I was for taking such a good nap. If she only knew…

Our New Car

I remember when we got our first new car (at least it was my first new car). It was a 1957 blue-and-white Chevrolet, and it was beautiful. I was sick the day my father brought it home. But after much begging and pleading, I got to go for a ride.

He drove up in front of the house like he was in a limousine. As I stood in the chair looking out the living room window, I thought, wow! The car was gleaming in the sunlight. It was really clean, I mean spic-and-span clean. The tail lights were recessed into what seemed like silver shark fins. And it had four doors. I couldn't wait to sit in the back seat.

My first ride consisted of going around the block. I think I had on my pajamas with a blanket wrapped around me. The ride was as smooth as an eagle gliding through the air. I waved to everyone on the street as we went by like I was on a float in a parade. I wanted them to know that we had a new car, and that I was proud.

My father drove that car like he was in the Indy 500. He would race and pass other cars, leaving them in the dust. First, he'd be in the inside lane, then he'd be in the outside lane, cutting off other drivers during the process. Sometimes, this would be at our urging. We'd say, "Come on, Daddy, pass that car. Go faster, Daddy, go faster." He'd always oblige much to our delight.

I remember him driving to Seattle for the World's Fair (1962). This meant going through the infamous Ellensburg Canyon. This canyon was narrow with winding roads that were quite dangerous. You'd be driving right next to a cliff. There was little room for error. The canyon had tunnels that were dark and scary. You had to be careful cuz' you never knew what was coming. A lot of big logging trucks used that canyon road, and they took up most of the room. There was plenty of honking going on.

This canyon proved to be a challenge for my father. He drove through it like a madman and refused to slow down for anything or anyone that crossed his path. I guess he figured anyone having the guts to drive through that canyon better have the guts to get out of his way! He would come so close to the shoulder, I swear we could stick out our arms and touch the rugged hillside next to us. I was always so scared. I don't remember much talking going on in the car while he was driving.

One time, we were riding through downtown Yakima. There was the Walnut Street tunnel that was a popular route. As we approached the tunnel, I stuck my head out of the window and yelled at the top of my lungs. It made an echo sound that was better than that made at the Grand Canyon. Of course, my father didn't quite see it that way. He asked me if I was crazy and told me to get my head (and other parts of my body) back in that car and never to do that again. I was so hurt. What harm had I done? Just because the entire universe could probably hear me…

Moma, on the other hand, drove very carefully and slowly. If she thought a car was following her too closely, she had two options: 1) either pull over and let the other car pass, or 2) stop suddenly to let the other car know she didn't appreciate the tailgating. It would be so embarrassing. I wanted to slide right under the seat so no one could see me in the car. But she meant business and was ready to get out and defend her action, if need be. I think she would have kicked some major butt, too!

That car went through heaven and hell. It was a good car and it lasted a long time. They don't build cars like that anymore. And my father stopped driving a long time ago.

Making Mud Pies

I remember making mud pies in our yard. Sometimes I would make them on the side of the house. Other times, I would make them in the front yard. Both were prime places, cuz' there was a water faucet and hose nearby, and the dirt in those locations was rich and had the right consistency.

I treated the dirt like flour. It had to be fine and free of any big rocks or pebbles. Those would ruin the batter for the pies. Since I wasn't allowed to use the flour sifter, I had to pick them out by hand. Plus, you had to make sure there weren't any bugs in the dirt. Ants, beetles, or worms were no good in my mud pies! I'd get enough dirt, assemble it in a pile, and slowly start adding the water. Some kids added the water all at one time, but I liked to add it slowly, mixing the dirt until it was just right. If you added too much water, the batter would be thin and runny. Then you'd have to add more dirt. You could mix the dirt with a stick or you could use your hands.

Once you had that part done, then came the kneading. Taking both hands, the soft, wet dirt could be rolled around into a ball. Then, with the palms of your hands you could press it out ever so gently until it was a larger, flatter ball of dough, evenly distributed for faster cooking. Now depending on how you wanted your pies to look, you could repeat this process several times.

If I wanted to make fancy mud pies, I would take some greenery (flowers or leaves) and mash it up until it was nicely ground. This then could be sprinkled on top as an added ingredient. It also gave the pies a nice bit of color.

By this time, you had to pay close attention to where the sun was. These pies had to bake properly and at the right temperature. It was no good if the sun was too hot. And, it wouldn't work if the shade moved in while you were mixing the pies. On several occasions, I had to move my pies after they were all assembled. That was tricky. I didn't have a spatula, but if I could find a sturdy piece of cardboard, I was in business.

It would behoove you to place the pies in a location off the main pathway. We didn't have pets, but my sisters' big feet had to be avoided. I would have died if anyone dared to step on my pies after all of that hard work. So they usually ended up against the side of the house. They would be all lined up like big cookies baking. I would be so proud.

After sitting in the sun for several hours, they had to be tested for doneness. This was accomplished by inserting a small twig into the pies. It they didn't break apart, or have unsightly cracks in them, you were good to go. Viewers could then be summoned to marvel over your masterpieces. I was an expert mud pie maker. I made them every day.

Apparently, making mud pies was an attribute handed down through the family. My oldest sister told me that when I first came home from the hospital with Moma, she had been making mud pies. She begged Moma to let her hold me saying, "Oh, Moma, let me hold the baby. Please, Moma, please." Moma told her she had to go wash her hands first. Can you just see it? Mud all over the new baby, all over me. Yuk.

You know, I don't think anyone ever volunteered to taste my mud pies. I don't remember if I ate them either. I guess some things are just for show.

ANTS

I remember when I used to play with all kinds of creatures, both living and dead. Maybe it was because we didn't have pets. Maybe it was because that's just what little kids do. I would dig the BBs out of dead birds (pretending to operate on them like Dr. Ben Casey). I would try to give CPR on small animals that got hit by cars. And, I would beg Moma to let me give milk to the stray cats that came to our back door. But I was most fascinated with ants. How did they make those anthills? And, why were some of them black while others were red? Were they like people? Did they fight with one another because the color of their bodies was different?

We had hedges around our yard, and they always had lots of spider webs in them. I used to get the black ants and put them in the spiders' webs. Then, I'd crouch down and wait patiently for the spider to come out from inside his house and do his thing. I think the spider could feel the movement of the ant being thrown into his web. If not, then he surely could feel the ant desperately trying to get away. Those legs would be flapping like clothes drying on the clothesline on a windy day. I don't know why they struggled so much, because they never got away. I was there to see to that. After all, the show would have been over had that happened.

The spider would usually appear from what seemed like this tunnel within his web. At first he wouldn't be visible, but then, slowly, he'd come creeping out. It appeared he would be looking all around and from side to side like a little kid watching out for cars before crossing the street. Was it a trick? Or, could it be a tender, sweet morsel waiting to be captured and eaten?

The spider would strike out like a snake. Then he'd start building this web around the ant so it couldn't get away. The web reminded me of a silkworm spinning silk. It was quite intricate. And if the sun was shinning just right, the web would take on the colors of the rainbow. It was a beautiful work of art. Probably not to the ant, though.

After the ant was secure, the spider would drag it into his tunnel. There, I assumed, the fine dining began. I wondered if they used catsup or mustard, or did they just eat the ant plain.

Now, the red ants were a different story. I usually didn't mess with them too much because they would sting you. And they were much bigger than the black ants too. I used to watch them hard at work on their anthills that were in the field next to our house. They were busy little critters. I'm not sure what they were doing, but they did a lot of it.

One day, for some unknown reason, I decided they were lonely. I remember lifting up my shirt and bending down in their anthill. I was going to give them a piggyback ride. I invited them all to climb aboard to have a little fun, promising not to run too fast for fear they would fall off and hurt themselves. Next thing I know, my back is on fire! I mean those ants were having a feast at my expense. I was screaming and running around like a chicken with its head cut off. I ran into the house shouting at the top of my lungs. Luckily, Moma was home. She looked at my back, which was in plain view cuz' I still had my shirt pulled over my head, and immediately put me in a tub of water. You should have seen all of those ants swimming around for their lives. They looked like salmon trying to swim upstream to spawn. Or like little kids when you first put them in a tub of water for their bath.

That was the last time I tried to make friends with those ants. Talk about ungrateful!

Grandmother

I remember spending a lot of time with Grandmother (Moma's mother). She used to baby-sit me while Moma worked. I guess my sisters would be at school.

I would stand up in the chair, which sat under the living room window, and wait for her to come walking down the sidewalk. When I finally spotted her, I think she could see me too cuz' she always started waving. I would run to the front door where she greeted me with a big hug.

Grandmother was real cool. She never got upset and she let me do most anything I wanted. The best part was the gum. She always had Juicy Fruit or Doublemint. I got to take my pick. Juicy Fruit usually won. It was so sweet it made my mouth water with delight. I would say, "Thank you, Grandmother." Then, she would say, "You're welcome, baby."

Grandmother had many husbands. I remember Papa Sam the most. He was the person who taught me about catsup. I don't know how that happened, but I loved the stuff. I used to eat catsup sandwiches. I'd pour the catsup right in the middle of the bread (and lots of it, too!). Then, I'd take a butter knife and smooth it all over until it covered every inch. I couldn't have any of the "white" in the bread showing. Then, I'd get a napkin, cuz' invariably some of the catsup would ooze out when I bit into the sandwich. It was fun to lick around the corners of the bread. That's where the extra catsup would be.

I used to eat my rice with margarine and sugar in it. Add a piece of toast, and I had a complete meal. One time, I had rice at Grandmother's house. But, something wasn't right. It tasted funny, and I didn't want to eat. She kept asking me what was wrong, but I couldn't explain it. The color was right. And so was the consistency. But, it just didn't taste the same. I finally figured out that Grandmother used "real" butter. We always used margarine. Who knew?

Grandmother used to have this dog named Chubby. He was a black-and-white collie (sort of like Lassie, only much better). I used to ride his back and kiss him on the lips. Chubby could walk to the store by himself, buy what Grandmother needed, and bring back the change. I loved that dog, and he loved me. Grandmother never had to worry about anybody messing with me while Chubby was around. He would have bitten their head clean off.

On time, Chubby and I were playing in Grandmother's back yard. She was pulling weeds. Her back yard seemed so big then. Chubby would be on one side of the yard, and I'd call him. He'd always come running to see what I wanted. Well, I never wanted anything. I just liked to call him. After he figured out that I didn't want anything, he would always run back to Grandmother. I did this over and over again. Grandmother told me to stop cuz' I was making Chubby tired. He didn't seem tired to me, but whatever. I could just look and wave to him, and he would still come running. He was a good playing buddy. And he was so obedient.

I remember when we had chickens in the back yard. Grandmother used to wring their necks until their heads came off. She could do it so good. One or two quick snaps of her wrist and that head was gone! It was so funny, cuz' even with their heads off those stupid chickens would still be running around the yard. Their big, ol' wings would be flapping while their little heads rested in the grass. I would always make sure to get out of their way. It was kinda like playing tag, only you never knew where those headless chickens would be running to next. I guess that's where they got the saying *running around like a chicken with its head cut off*. I think this whole process made either my brother or my sister sick to the stomach. They refused to eat chicken after witnessing that cruel execution. I didn't mind though, especially if the chicken was fried. I liked the skin the best.

I don't remember Grandmother ever reading to me, but she sure had great stories. According to her, she was a bad actor. Being four-foot-eleven, I guess she had to be. She was a feisty little lady. She told me stories of when she pulled out her switchblade (from her bosom) and jumped on somebody, some man. She was always threatening to cut somebody's throat for messing with her. And I believe she would have done it, too. She told me once that she got kicked out of the state of Arkansas and was told never to come back. Now, I had heard of people getting kicked out of school, but a whole state? I pictured her face on one of those *Wanted Dead or Alive* posters. I wondered what they would have done if she did show up again. Would they shoot her? Would they put her in jail? My Grandmother…a criminal.

After I got older, she used to say things to me that were just incredible. She told me that I was grown now, and I knew what she was talking about, didn't I? How could I deny it? I knew exactly what she was talking about. It was just that I was shocked that she was saying it! She would always be talking about her *nature* saying she had no use for men anymore cuz' she was too old. One time she told me this man wanted to see her, but she said she didn't need him. She said, "I don't care if he shit silver dollars and had a gold ring around his dick, I still wouldn't let him near me, Baby." Well, I fell out laughing trying to picture this scene in my mind. Was there such a thing as a gold dick ring? And why wouldn't she want those silver dollars? She could spend them just like any other money.

Today, Grandmother is in her 90s and lives in a nursing home. But I think she is still wreaking havoc. I can see her now, walking down the hall threatening to cut anyone that dares mess with her (even if there isn't anyone around!). I'm sure she doesn't get any takers. Bad Leroy Brown didn't have anything on Grandmother; no one did.

The First Grade

I remember when I started going to school. I didn't go to kindergarten (something to do with when my birthday fell), so I started off in the first grade.

I was really apprehensive (I was scared) because I didn't know what to expect. I'm sure I cried because I didn't want to go. I had just gotten used to staying at home, and now I had to go to school. My sister would walk with me on her way to junior high. I used to beg her to come and visit me during her lunch. But she always said she couldn't. Didn't she get recess? Couldn't she come to visit me then? Apparently not.

First grade was quite the experience. We had these little desks that had little chairs connected to them. There was a big, black chalkboard in the front of the room, and the teacher's desk was up there, too. My teacher's name was Mrs. Duntley. She was the nicest woman you ever wanted to meet. She was kind and never yelled at us, no matter what we did.

One time we all had to take turns getting up in front of the class and counting as far as we could go. On this particular day, it was my turn. I remember getting to about 20 with no problem and then I went astray. Then it was 35, 22, 99, 87, and the final, ultimate number, 100. The teacher said I did good and could take my seat.

Moma used to sew all of my clothes, and my hair was usually combed in two ponytails or French braids. I always got to have bangs, though. And, most of the time, I had ribbons in my hair. My sisters had the responsibility of combing my hair before I went to school (Moma had to work and left before we did). Sometimes, instead of combing my hair right, they would put lots of Bobby pins in it to hold it down (not that my hair was unruly, or anything). The next day, before combing it, all of the Bobby pins would have to be removed. I can remember having as many as 15 on one side of my head. Good thing they were black. That way you couldn't tell how many were there. I was the Bobby pin queen!

Sometimes, the whole class would march down to the auditorium to see films. Everyone had to walk in an orderly fashion (single file). My favorite film was *Our Mr. Sun*. I loved this film because it was educational, teaching us all about the sun. We learned about the sun's temperature and how close it was to the moon and other planets. The colors were bold and beautiful. We all sat on the floor with our legs crossed gazing endlessly at the big screen in front.

Moma used to send me to school with my lunch money tied up in a hanky. This was so I wouldn't lose it on the way. Then she would use a safety pin and secure the money safely on the inside of my skirt. The problem was she would tie two or three knots around the money to keep it from falling out. And I could never get the knots out! I would struggle with it every day. Finally, she got enough money so that I could buy lunch tickets for the entire week. What a relief!

I wore those God-awful saddle shoes, black and white. No matter how much I kicked at the dirt and ground, I could never wear those bad boys out. They were built to last a lifetime. Every now and then, I'd get to polish them. We would all polish our shoes at the same time (with that white polish that came in a little jar with the applicator that had the pom-pom brush on the end). Then, we'd line them up against the wall on a piece of newspaper to dry.

I usually wore these little skirts with suspenders and a blouse. All of the patterns were the same, but I did get to have different color material. I can remember Moma staying up all night sewing and then getting up and going to work the next morning. But, our clothes were always clean, well sewn, and neat.

The first grade really wasn't that bad. But what I didn't realize was that I would be going to school for what seemed like the rest of my life!

Tip, Spot, Dick, and Jane

I remember when I began entering the world of "reading." I must have been in the first or second grade. I loved reading as my imagination could take over, and it was okay. One of my favorite books was about an unorthodox family that consisted of two dogs (Tip and Spot), a brother (Dick), and a sister (Jane). Who knows where their parents were or who took care of them. These were the only characters in the whole book (or at least the only ones I cared about).

I used to come home reading that book. I was so excited and wanted to read to everyone. My mother was the most attentive audience. I read my heart out to her. When she got tired of me reading (although, she never let on that she was sick of hearing me read), she would send me off to my sisters. I was so proud of myself because when I read aloud in school, the teacher said I read with expression. You would think I was trying out for a major part in a movie. My sisters didn't want to hear about Tip, Spot, or anybody else that I thought was interesting, but Moma made them. She would always say, "Listen to the baby read. She reads with expression."

I can still remember the lines, "See Tip run. Run, Tip, run. See Dick throw the ball to Tip. See Jane play with Spot." I made those characters come to life when I read. My voice inflections were perfect. I read those lines as if they were from Shakespeare and I was a thespian. I always stood up straight when I read. My posture was good, and I held the book just so (although, I'm sure I had it memorized). I would walk back and forth as if I was on stage doing a monologue. I would look up every now and then to focus on my audience. I needed to see if I had captured their attention.

Usually, all I captured was my sisters making faces, rolling their eyes, and wondering if I was done yet.

That book was action packed. Everybody was always doing something. Tip and Spot would be running around like wild animals. They could jump over bushes, hide under porches, and run after balls and sticks. Dick and Jane would be busy trying to catch them or make them do some kind of dumb trick. No wonder those poor dogs would be trying to hide! Did they ever get any rest? I don't remember them ever eating either. But, they did seem to be happy.

I think the teacher gave us the homework assignment of reading to our family. Then, the next day we would have to get up in front of the class and read aloud. You could always tell who had practiced the night before and who hadn't. There was this one boy, Mike, who couldn't read worth beans. He would always get certain words mixed up—words like who, how, what, why, and where. I used to get so frustrated listening to him read. Didn't he know how to sound out words? And yet the teacher would always call on him. Every time it was his turn to read, all of the other kids would start moaning. We knew it was torture time with Mike. I used to ask him at recess why he always got the words mixed up. I wanted to know just what the problem was. I don't remember what he said, but he was a nice boy so I let him slide. Maybe his Moma didn't make his sisters listen to him read. Maybe he didn't even have a Moma.

To this day, I still have a problem listening to others read aloud. I can't stand it when people fumble over words or read without expression. Don't they know they are on stage? Don't they know they are putting on a performance for the critics? I wish I had kept that book about Tip, Spot, Dick, and Jane. I know a few people who could use it.

The Uncle Jimmy Show

I remember on my seventh birthday, I got to go on "The Uncle Jimmy Show." This was a momentous occasion that I'll never forget. "The Uncle Jimmy Show" was a local syndicated television program that celebrated children's birthdays. I had often watched this program at home. There were cartoons on the show and all of these kids who were having birthdays. The kids would get cake, Uncle Jimmy would talk to each one of them, and then everybody sang happy birthday. The best part was that you got to be on TV.

Well, now it was my turn. I couldn't believe I was actually going on the show. I was going to be on TV and everything! My mother told everyone in town. All eyes were going to be on me. I had a new dress, and my hair was combed just right. I even had new ribbons in my hair. I think I also had new shoes, although they didn't show anyone's feet on "The Uncle Jimmy Show."

The big day finally arrived. We got to the TV station in plenty of time. I was so nervous. What was I going to say to Uncle Jimmy? Would he get my name right? I felt like I was going to be sick.

There was this big, long table that all of the birthday guests had to sit behind. There were lots of TV cameras and bright lights. And, right in the middle of the room was the biggest birthday cake I had ever seen. I wondered if they were actually going to cut that cake and let us eat it. Then I wondered if the cake was even real. Somebody was going to give me some birthday cake before I left that TV station.

Right before the program went on the air, I noticed this fly had landed on the cake. He was walking around like he was a runway model. Didn't he know that was MY birthday cake? I did not want his germs on my piece. After all, who knows where he had been? He'd walk around, then fly away. He'd come back, fly around the cake and then sit on it. I was fascinated with this fly. Why wasn't anyone shooing the thing away? Were they just going to let him walk all over it? It was like I was hypnotized by the fly. I couldn't take my eyes off him. I followed his every move on that cake. I wondered if the people watching TV could see the fly. Did they know what I was looking at? Were they going to try to give me the piece of cake that the fly landed on? I had seen flies land on dog poop in the yard and other nasty stuff including dead things. I had no intention of eating any of that cake. Why was this happening to me? I had finally gotten on "The Uncle Jimmy Show" and this fly was ruining it!

You know, after the show I don't remember if Uncle Jimmy got my name right or what he even said to me. I asked my sister what I said, and she told me that I announced to everyone that I was seven years old, but that I was speaking very softly. She thought it was because I was shy in front of the TV cameras. I think I told her about the fly, although her reaction was nothing like mine. I guess you had to be there.

There was another momentous occasion on my seventh birthday. I have to admit, however, it is more meaningful now than then.

There was this old woman who lived at the very end of the next block from our house. Her house was as old as she, and both were very scary. There were overgrown weeds and grass in her yard, and it made her house look like it was haunted. We would always run past her house for fear that something (or someone) might start chasing us.

Mrs. McVey (the old woman that lived in the old house) gave me a plaque for my seventh birthday. She wrote my name and the date on the back. It was wooden with two little yellow ducks on it. And, it had pink flowers on it, too. It said, "I will trust and not be afraid." (Psalms 56:4 & 11; Isaiah 12:2)

I still have that plaque today. And I can still make out some of her handwriting on the back. It is in my bedroom on a glass shelf in plain view. I will keep it forever and remember that all is not as it may seem.

WEARING GLASSES

I remember when I first started wearing glasses. I think I was in the second or third grade. My father wore glasses, Moma wore glasses, I think my brother wore glasses, and two of my three sisters wore glasses. I guess it was just a matter of time before it was my turn.

My first pair was plaid frames. Now I know you are thinking "yuk," but these glasses were cool. They were blue, red, yellow, and green. And they matched every outfit I wore! I'm sure the frames were hand-me-downs. But that didn't matter cuz' now they were *mine*. Then, there were the white, cat-eyed glasses. Moma had them, two of my three sisters had them, and I had them. You could see us coming for miles. We were stars in *the invasion of the white, cat-eyed glasses* drama.

It's amazing, but I didn't get teased too much in school about having to wear glasses. Rarely did I get called four-eyes (that came later). To the contrary, everyone wanted to try them on. They wanted to see what I saw and how I saw it. They wanted to see how my eyes were different from theirs. It was as though I had something very special that they didn't have.

Some of the kids' heads would be too big and my glasses would fit funny. One side would go around one of their ears the way it should, but the other side would be all cock-eyed. The part that should have gone around their other ear would end up around the side of their head instead! I'd have to tell them to take my glasses off before they stretched them out. Other kids would put them on and say, "Whooa, I can really see good with these! Where'd you get them?" I'd have to explain that my glasses were *not* purchased off the shelf in a grocery store. I'd tell them that a doctor examined my eyes and prescribed the lenses especially for me. The concept of frames versus lenses was not clear to them. They only thought of glasses, period.

My eyes were so bad that I had to put my glasses on first thing in the morning. I couldn't go to the bathroom without them. I couldn't see the clock without them. I couldn't read without them. Sometimes, I would take my glasses off and try squinting to see if I could focus clearly. I ended up looking like a rat sniffing out a piece of cheese. And I still couldn't see. Everything would be all blurry, and I eventually would get a headache. It's so weird when the whole world is fuzzy. I could see large shapes, but I couldn't make out what the big blob was supposed to be.

Keeping my glasses clean was another challenge. I couldn't understand what all that stuff on them was. And I really couldn't understand how it all got there. I was pretty neat, and most of the time I was indoors, so I couldn't blame it on the wind. I'd take them off and hold them directly in front of my eyes thinking I could figure out what all that foreign matter was. Rarely did that happen. The stuff on my glasses just looked like a bunch of stuff. Sometimes, I could see pieces of hair, but usually it was globs of smear and other particles. I would think, "Lordy, what is all of this?" If they hadn't been on my face, I would have been afraid to touch them.

I used to spit on my glasses to clean them. Then, I would wipe them on my blouse or some other part of my clothing. That didn't work too well. I'd end up not being able to see anything. Then, I began using alcohol. That, and a piece of toilet tissue. The best solution seemed to be a smidge of dishwashing liquid and a paper towel. My glasses would be sparkling, and I would be ever so happy. It was like seeing things clearly again for the first time. It was like a sunny day with blue skies and big, white clouds breaking out from the gloom and doom of darkness and rain.

I still wear glasses. I've contemplated contact lenses or even laser surgery. But I still have my four eyes. I even have more than one pair. I have sunglasses too, red frames in the shape of an octagon. And, you know what? Plaid is in!

Going to Church

I remember going to church every Sunday. There was Sunday School that started around 8:30a.m., and then there was the morning worship service that started around 11:00a.m.

Sunday service was pretty organized. We had an adult choir, a young adult choir, and a children's choir (the Cherub Choir cuz' we were little angles!). The adult choir had a pianist who was also the choir director. She played really well. I liked it because she put a little beat in the hymns. I can still hear the introductory theme, "God of Our Fathers." When this hymn started, the adult choir members would come marching in from the rear on both sides of the church. It seemed so heavenly, and they certainly commanded the attention of the congregation. We all had to stand during the commencement. They filed in, one by one, and marched right up to the choir loft. They wore black-and-white robes that were long and flowing. Their heads were held high, and their voices filled the church. It was like they were singing to God.

There was this one man who often sang solos. His voice was smooth, yet compelling. When he sang, you were filled with the Spirit. Usually, people would start crying. I guess the reaction could be compared to that of when Frank Sinatra or Nat King Cole sang. I used to get chills listening to him. It was incredible (plus, he was good looking). He should have been on the radio or making records. He was that good. His most memorable hymn was, "There Will Be Peace In The Valley."

Now when the preaching started, it was a different story. The minister would always start off rather calm and then build up to a mighty crescendo! He put on quite a performance. Everyone would be shouting, "Amen" or "Preach it, Brother." Sometimes you would hear, "Now that's awright" or "Yeesss, Lawd" and "Thank ya, Jesssus!" He would be jumping up and down and waving his hands around like someone who was lost on a deserted island trying to attract the attention of a rescue plane. He would sweat profusely. One of the deaconesses always had to take the infamous white hanky and wipe his forehead. I used to think, "ugh, all that sweat." Then I used to wonder if he smelled afterwards.

Where you sat during the church service was very important. Why, you ask? The answer was because of Sister Townes. She was a good, kind woman. And she was very large! She would always get filled with the Holy Ghost, and the shouting would begin. I don't mean just screaming real loud. I mean full-blown shouting! You could always tell when this was about to happen. She would be singing, and then all of a sudden her shoulders would begin to shake. You knew the transformation was about to take place. She would start crying, and her arms would be waving like an ostrich frantically trying to fly. Used to scare me to death. If you were so unlucky as to sit anywhere within two pews of Sister Townes, you were likely to get knocked out by those flying arms. They were like enormous hams with wings; you know, the kind you bought for Easter dinner. Her punch was fiercer than anything Mohammed Ali could even think about throwing. It would take at least two or three deacons and three or four deaconesses to calm her down and get her out of the church. Man, it was frightening! I didn't understand for a long time what was going on. All I knew was that it was dangerous sitting anywhere near that woman. She seemed so normal before church service started. Sometimes, she would even have candy.

Then, there was Sister Payne. I remember the first time I sat behind her. I was looking around, not paying attention as usual, when I first saw them. I couldn't believe my eyes! There were these little, pointy claws around her neck. I sat up straight so I could get a closer look. I couldn't quite figure it out, so I decided to follow the little claws from the pointy nails all the way around her neck. It was hard to do because there was so much brown fur. Her skin was smooth and brown, too, and it was a challenge to tell where the fur ended and her skin began. Well, my eyes traveled slowly and deliberately until I saw the small, black, shiny eyes sitting in its head. What the?! Seems as though she had on a small fox stole. I had only seen one on TV and never close up. I wanted to touch it so bad, but I was scared. On top of that, she probably would have told on me.

After church, everyone would hug and kiss everybody else. I used to wonder why. We saw each other every Sunday. It's not like it had been years! The worst part was when one of the sisters of the church hugged you. They had some big breasts (or titties as we referred to them back then). It was like being smothered in super-duper sized down pillows. You were buried for at least 30 seconds. I finally learned to hold my breath. It was the only hope for survival.

But, I always knew Sunday dinner would be waiting. The food was spread out like the king was coming. And you could always eat as much as you wanted. It made everything worthwhile. To that I said, "Amen."

Bible Study

I remember going to bible study with my sisters. I loved going because we would always learn things about God, Jesus, and what the bible said. We were learning about the gospel, and though I didn't know it at the time, this experience was further building a foundation that would be with me for the rest of my life.

We could walk to bible study because this lady that lived around the corner from us held it at her house. I usually skipped or ran because I wanted to be one of the first ones there. I think we went about once a week or so. My memories must have focused around the winter months. I say that because going over there it would be dark and sometimes chilly. Everyone had sweaters or coats.

I remember this lady's house being quite small. There were lots of children, and some of us would always have to sit on the floor. But we didn't care. We were just glad to be there. Her house was always warm, and sometimes we had hot chocolate, and sometimes we had cookies.

I vaguely remember her using a felt board that was used to display bible figures or certain scriptures. It was so cool because stuff seemed to stick to it like magic. Nothing ever fell off, and everyone in the room could see. She told stories and read to us from the bible. We got to ask questions and sing songs too. Sometimes we would have contests to see who could memorize scriptures or bible verses and explain what they meant. I think it was there that I memorized the Twenty-third Psalm.

I particularly like that scripture because it is so calming and serene. It has always given me the feeling of someone or something being so caring and loving and watching over me. It makes me feel as if all is peaceful, and the need to worry doesn't exist. There is compassion and sincerity. That's how I felt about bible study too. At the end of every bible study we held hands and prayed. We were safe and happy.

This woman always welcomed us in her house. It was like we were all her children and she was happy to see us. She was so kind. I don't think we ever stayed to help her clean up (at least I didn't). Nor did we ever give her any money that I knew of. Maybe we took up an offering, which couldn't have consisted of more than some small pocket change cuz' that's all we had. I don't remember where she came from or what happened to her afterwards. It was as if she was our guardian angel.

Sometimes, I still go to bible study. But it's different now. It seems like everyone is always trying to make a point about what THEY think the scripture says. There are arguments over whether the term "man" used in the bible refers to men and women or if it is just a sexist interpretation of the author. There are wise cracks over the fact that wisdom takes on the feminine gender and that men would do well to pay closer attention to women (or what, go to hell?). There is resentment over passages that say women should consider their husbands as their masters (maybe that's why I'm not married cuz' ain't no man gonna tell me what to do!).

Don't get me wrong, these points are valid and serve as good discussion points. However, it saddens me when I think back on the feeling I used to get from going to bible study as a child and the feelings I leave with now. There is something to be said for having a child-like innocence. It's a different kind of attitude that allows the mind the freedom to absorb without prejudice or suspicion. It's a different kind of attitude that can allow for wonderful memories.

Nick Names

I remember having a lot of nicknames when I was young. You see I was very fat, and most of my nicknames reflected that fact. Someone told me I was so fat that I reminded them of a tub of lard. So, I got the nickname Tub-o-lard. Then, as a variation of that, I got called Tubby. There was also Lard Bucket. My brother used to call me Annie Horse (cuz' my middle name is Ann and I was as big as a horse). Except when he called me that, I knew it was a term of endearment rather than an insult. He would have never done anything to hurt me. I can't say the same for two of my sisters.

My sisters were so mean to me. They used to sit me in a chair in the middle of the living room. Then they would run around the chair like Indians with tomahawks in their hands yelping and whooping about how fat I was. Out of their mouths would come the song, "Fatty, fatty, two-by-four. Couldn't get through the bathroom door." Other times, when we would be walking home together, they would run ahead of me, turn around, pointing and shouting, "She's not our sister. We don't know her." I would cry every day behind something they were saying about me. But my oldest sister made up for all of their teasing. She would get a broom, chase them out of the house, and lock the door. That made me feel better. She would always tell me that she loved me and not to pay attention to those other two. Easier said than done.

When I was in elementary school, I hung out with a girl friend that lived around the corner from us. Her name was Doris. She and her family were from the South and pronounced words a little differently than us. Every time her younger sister would see me coming around the corner to pick her up, she would call to Doris saying, "Daaws, hea com Beah." To this day one of my sisters still calls me Beah (another term of endearment).

My mother used to call me "Baby" unless I was in trouble, then it was Vetress. My grandmother used to call me Vetress Ann or sometimes "The Baby" (as if I wasn't in the room). My father would call me all of my other sisters' names. I think he would just forget who was who (or who he was trying to summon at the time, cuz' none of us would respond when he called. We thought that was so funny!).

Today, one of my sisters calls me "Ponchita." I think at one time she had a neighbor named "Lorita." Then, we noticed an actress named Maria "Conchita" Alonso. So, I ended up being Ponchita. I have a niece that calls me Beatree. This is because so many people think my name is Beatrice. So she always says to me, "Hi Beatree. Be-a-tree, not a flower, Be-a-tree." Now, her daughter calls me that too. She thinks that name is so funny, but at five you think just about everything is funny.

I've been call Citrus, Deirdre, Vernita, Venus, and numerous other names. However, I think those were misunderstandings rather than nicknames.

The one nickname that is pretty much universal is "Dee Dee." My family has always called me that, and now some of my friends do too. I've been asked, how do you get Dee Dee out of Vetress? Well, when I came home from the hospital one of my sisters tried to say "Vetress" and it came out "Vee Vee" or "Dee Dee" instead. That's been my nickname since. I am also called just "Dee" (as well as other names, I'm sure).

My brother James used to be called Buddy-fat or Bubba. My sister Cherry is Chair-ko-day. Now I call her Miss Cherry. So do her students and some of the people at her church. My sister Ruby is Ruberto or Ruby-duby. Her husband Moses is Mo-zeke-a-row (Moma made that one up). I once had a friend whose first and last name were names of presidents. Moma used to call him Grover Cleveland (only that wasn't his name!). And, my sister Linda is Lean-der (she said a woman of Asian decent called her that once). My niece Stacy is Fayda Jane, and my nephew Harry is Fuug. My other niece Dione is Own-bone or O-nay-ho. Remember

Parliament and Funk-a-delic? They used the phrase, "Uh, Rowda Rooda Baby" in one of their songs. So, now I call certain people Rowda Rooda (including me when I talk to myself!).

    Isn't it funny how nicknames get attached to people? Think about it. What are your nicknames and from where did they originate? Do you know? Ask somebody.

CELEBRITIES

I remember when Little Richard used to get his hair done three doors down from where we lived. When I say, "get his hair done" it means someone was putting chemicals (bad smelling chemicals) on it to straighten it. Or someone was using a hot comb (an iron comb that was heated on the stove top until it was red-hot) and straightening his hair, also known as "pressing hair." Now, hopefully, this someone was either a bonafide hair stylist or at the very least knew what they were doing. If not, the results could be devastating, not to mention the fact that you could end up looking like sin.

You see, even then Little Richard was famous. We used to get so excited when he came. Not only was he nice, everybody knew who he was, and he would give us money! We would run down to Mrs. Kyle's house (that was the lady that did hair. She was good, too!) like little heathens when we knew Little Richard was there. Though, I don't think he ever sang for us, he did talk to us. I don't remember him ever chasing us away. We must have been like little magpies running all around and talking to him at once. We were in heaven.

My sister later told me that Jackie Wilson used to get his hair done there as well. I don't remember that part, but it does make sense. They both wore the same kind of style: long, high, and swooped up in front. Their hair would be shinning like new money (coins of course). I never thought of this before; however, they must have used some serious hair spray, cuz' even with all that movin and groovin they would be doing, that hair stayed in place. Either that or they had some serious grease on it (oh, excuse me, I mean pomade). I loved Jackie Wilson's songs, "Just a kiss, just a smile, hold me darling just once in a while. That's all I need and I'll be satisfied." Humph, too bad that formula doesn't work today!

My sisters used to get to go to these dances. Sometimes they would be held at the Armory (just down the street from our house) on Third Street, and sometimes they would be held at this place in Wapato (pronounced Wap'a'toe), a small town about 12 miles from Yakima where we lived. Sometimes my father would drive them, and I would get to ride along. I remember Fats Domino would play there all the time. Of course, I never saw him, but my sisters would tell me all about him. I knew all the words to his songs. "I found my thril-l-l on Blueberry Hil-l-l." And then there was this song "I want to walk you home. Please let me walk you home." I used to pretend I was Fats Domino and play the piano just like him and sing. Come to think of it, he had that slicked-back hair too. I wonder if he ever got his hair done by our house?

The celebrities fascinated me. These were the same people I'd see on TV and hear on the record player. I wondered how they got so famous? I wondered how much money they had? I wondered where their families were? I wondered why they came to Yakima to get their hair done?

Having famous people come to town made me feel famous too. I would go to school and proudly announce to everybody, "I talked to Little Richard, and my sisters saw Fats Domino." They probably didn't even know who I was talking about, but that didn't matter. The way I was strutting around they knew something important had happened and that I was a part of it! And of course when it came to sharing time, I'd get up in front of the class and tell all about the celebrities that were in my neighborhood. Those were the good old days. You think Little Richard remembers that now? I'd love to ask him. Well, do you, Little Richard?

Asthma Attacks

I remember being sick a lot; you see, I had asthma. I was always having asthma attacks. My nose would get all stuffed up, and I couldn't breathe. I would have a temperature and cough my head off. I would sneeze and wheeze all day and all night long. I missed a lot of school during the year.

Moma used to take good care of me. When I had a temperature, she would put me in the tub with cool water. And then sometimes she would alternate that by filling the tub with warm water. I used to have to take this medicine that was thick and yellow. It tasted really bad, but it was a deep, rich, beautiful yellow color, kinda' like a sunflower. I think it was a prescription antihistamine. I would have to take one full tablespoon several times a day. I hated that medicine. And I kept getting sick, so was it doing any good?

When I got sick I'd have to stay in bed. Sometimes, Moma would let me lay on the couch and watch TV. I liked that. She'd have the vaporizer going, Kleenex on the coffee table, a waste paper basket, and 7-Up handy. I had everything I needed. Every now and then she would come over and take my temperature. She stroked my forehead and ask me if I felt better. She'd say, "Does my baby feel any better?" I'd whimper back (like a little puppy), "A little bit, Moma." I'd be sick as a dog, but feeling oh so loved.

The thing about asthma is it's very difficult to breathe. I was always fascinated by the fact that I was so plugged up and couldn't breathe out of my nose. Sometimes I could only breathe out of one nostril. When this happened, I'd plug the good nostril with one finger to see just how bad it was. Could any air get through the bad nostril at all? Nope. But, if I blew hard enough, my ears would pop. Other times I couldn't breathe out of my nose at all. I'd have to breathe out of my mouth. This left my mouth as dry as when I used to eat flour. Then my throat would get all scratchy (like a brillo pad), and I'd be coughing my fool head off.

My mother could always tell when I was getting sick. First, she would smell my breath (eewww!). I can't image what that told her other than I had halitosis. Then, she would look into my eyes and feel my forehead. I knew the thermometer was next. And, finally, the yellow medicine. What torture, what pain.

Having asthma really put a damper on my social life. I couldn't be around dogs or cats (not that I liked them that much anyway, except for Chubby, my grandmother's dog. He was like Lassie.). Fresh cut grass would kill me. The smell of cigarette smoke made me wheeze instantly. And dust would do me in without fail. My eyes would start tearing-up like someone had really hurt my feelings. Then they'd get all red. My head would get clogged worse than any plugged drain. I'm sure I looked a mess.

One time I was at home sick, and it had snowed. It snowed at lot in Yakima, like three and four feet at a time. Now, I loved to make angels in the snow. Yep, you guessed it. I was outside making angels in the snow when I was supposed to be in bed. I tried to explain to Moma that the angels I made that day were some of the best ever. The wing span was incredible! I don't think I got a whuppin', but she certainly wasn't happy with me.

For the most part, I think I grew out of my asthma attacks. But, to this day, cigarette smoke makes me wheeze instantly, dogs and cats make my nose plug up, and fresh cut grass sends a signal from my brain to my eyes to start the tears. Sometimes I start wheezing after I drink beer (gotta' be the hops). I feel really badly for the young folk today with asthma. I'm more than sure they don't get the love and care I got from Moma. Today, they have inhalers, which is certainly no substitute.

GET THE SOAP

I remember whenever we said something derogatory, looked less than angelic, or walked like we thought we were "all that," Moma would wash our mouths out with soap. Not just any soap, Ivory soap (the one that floats). Well, I'm here to tell you that soap was the nastiest tasting stuff I've ever had in my mouth (next to okra, and okay, a few other things…).

The bad thing was, yooou had to go get the soap. And, then she'd tell you to open wide so the whole bar would fit inside. Now you know how wide Ivory soap is. Moma would stick the entire bar in your mouth, and then move it around in circles as if to actually wash the filth away. By the time she was finished you could blow bubbles just by trying to breathe.

If you called someone a liar, you got your mouth washed out with soap. If you cussed, you got your mouth washed out with soap and got a whuppin'. If Moma told you to do something and you had that "look" on your face, you got your mouth washed out with soap. If you mumbled under your breath, you got your mouth washed out with soap. Getting the picture? Even your friends were in danger of getting their mouths washed out with soap if they didn't act right. Moma didn't discriminate.

Once you had the opportunity to taste the soap, it seemed like you could never get rid of it. No amount of toothpaste or mouthwash could make it go away. It made your whole mouth slimy. Not only that, it got all over your teeth so that when you ran your tongue over them tiny bits of soap taste still emerged. Afterwards, looking in the mirror, you could see the white film all around your mouth. It would be all sticky like snot. You ended up looking like Al Jolson. When you took a bath, it was hard to use that same soap to wash your body with, knowing you had just had the pleasure of washing out your mouth. I often wondered if the soap contained some kind of chemicals that were harmful if swallowed (I always meant to look at the package for those warnings, but who would think?).

I used to imagine gagging and having to go to the hospital for emergency surgery. That would make Moma feel real bad. Then she would have to tell the doctor what happened. This wasn't just a stupid child that decided to eat soap instead of dinner. Noooo, Moma made me eat the soap. I wondered if they would put her in jail for this. What would we do if Moma went to jail? I decided that probably wasn't a good idea.

And, then there were those times I wondered if you got your mouth washed out too many times would you be able to float like the soap did in the bathtub. That always amazed me. How did they make the soap do that? No other soap floated like that. Actually, it was kind of cool. Whenever you dropped the soap in the bath water, you never had to feel around to find it. It always popped back up to the surface.

Did other people get their mouths washed out with soap? I didn't dare ask, cuz' what if they didn't? They'd be asking me why I wanted to know. They'd be asking me if I got my mouth washed out with soap. They'd be laughing at me. I couldn't have that. I decided I could smell their breath to see if it had that telltale soap smell. But, then looking at some of my friends' teeth, I thought better of that idea.

Speaking of teeth, ours were probably the cleanest in town. People would say, "There goes those Arnold girls. They have such nice smiles." I guess that soap was good for something after all.

To this day, I still don't call people liars. And, I don't use Ivory soap.

Abuse

I remember abuse running rampant throughout my family while growing up. I'm talking about physical abuse as well as verbal abuse. My reactions to this violence included sympathy, anger, depression, and fear, just to name a few. I vowed never to engage in that kind of behavior no matter what.

It started with my mother and father. They mostly fought over money matters. And then there was a question of fidelity on my father's part. It had something to do with him buying a trailer for that woman who lived down the street.

My parents fought physically. One time my mother had taken a punch to her mouth, and her front teeth were bleeding. I remember her being in our bedroom crying softly. For some reason I was in there with her and was crying just like she was. I was patting her on the arm and chanting, "Please don't cry. It will be alright." I wanted her to know that I understood and was feeling the same pain. We didn't really talk, nor did she touch me in any way. We just sat on the bed and cried softly together. I remember walking out of the back door with her. She found her way to the garden, and there she spat out the excess blood from her mouth. I saw her deep, red blood on the green strawberry leaves glistening in the sun like rare rubies. That's probably why the strawberries were so vibrantly red and sweet that year.

Mostly, my parents fought in their room. I really couldn't see them fighting, but I could hear them. I think that was worse, as my imagination had full reign over what was going on. I could tell when it was really bad because I heard their bodies knocking against the walls and the other furniture in the room. It sounded like thunder rumbling or a train coming down the railroad tracks like the one in the back of our house. I could hear the punches landing, the cries of pain, the cussing, and the screaming.

Even though my father was well over six feet and my mother was only five-three, she held her own. Sometimes she would launch a full-blown attack like a lion stalking prey for a kill. She'd be sitting there one minute quiet and poised. She would have this sinister gleam in her eye focusing in on the target (daddy). And, then before you knew what happened, she'd be on him going for his jugular. The element of surprise was crucial. It all happened so fast and with such precision. I often wondered if he was afraid. I certainly was!

One time, daddy was sitting in the living room. He and Moma were arguing about something. Suddenly she threw this bottle of dishwashing liquid at him. It hit the wall behind the TV and left a blue-green waterfall pattern. No one ever cleaned it up.

The fighting didn't stop with my mother and father. Oh, no. Two of my sisters fought with their husband as well, and in the same house. One of my sisters used to fight with her husband while she was pregnant. I always wondered why my father never stopped them. How could they be fighting with a baby insider her? What was the baby thinking? I was so afraid that the baby would get hurt. This sister used to drive around town looking for her husband. As soon as she spotted him, it was on! She would jump out of the car and on him.

My oldest sister got her share of knocks as well. Even before she married her abusive husband, Big Larry, he was beating her. He was aptly named Big Larry because he was a huge man. One night he came over while Moma wasn't home. At the time, my sister had been seeing this guy who lived down the street. Big Larry knocked on the door, all proper, asking to see my sister. I told her not to go outside. I told her he was going to beat her up. Well, she went outside anyway, and sure enough, he started punching on her like one of those fighting kangaroos on cartoons. The guy she was dating tried to sneak away, but Big Larry caught him by the pants and threw him in the hedges (after picking him up and ramming his head into the big tree in the front yard. You know, like on the Three Stooges). I hated Big Larry for beating my sister. I wanted to kill him for hurting her. I begged her not to marry him. But she married him anyway.

When I got older, I dated a couple of guys who bragged about beating their women. I remember telling one of them if he ever hit me, he'd better kill me cuz' *he* would be dead if he didn't. For some reason, I never had that problem.

Playing in the Basement

I remember spending a lot of time playing in our basement. It was like having my own playhouse right in the house. I could go down there and play to my heart's content, and no one would bother me. I don't think they ever missed me. I don't think they even knew where I was or what I was doing.

There were lots of interesting things in the basement. That is, if you had an active imagination and no one else to play with.

We had a washing machine, but I don't think we had a dryer. There was, however, a clothesline that Moma had strung so certain clothes could hang dry. Otherwise, we hung our clothes outside in the warm, fresh air. Moma used to wash her bras by hand or on the gentle cycle in the washer. She would then hang them on the clothesline downstairs with clothespins to secure them. The thing about her bras was that they were huge! I remember looking at the size once and seeing nothing but EE or EEE. I was amazed. I knew her breasts were big, but YIKES!! I could fit one cup on my entire head. I used to walk around downstairs with her bra on my head. Then I'd put it on my chest and pretend I was an opera singer. That particular charade was very appropriate because of the bra's pointy cups.

We also had a coal bin in the basement. When it was time to fill up the bin, a big truck would come to our house, insert this chute-like instrument from the window in the back yard, and the black coal would come rushing right into the coal bin. I remember the coal being jet black, and it would always glisten in the light like black diamonds. There was a Stoka (I think that was the brand name) furnace next to the coal bin. You would shovel the coals into the hot, burning Stoka furnace, and that is what heated our house. I always liked to open the furnace and shovel in the coals, cuz' it would be so hot. That fire would be roaring, and it reminded me of what it must have been like for Shadrach, Meshach, and Abed-nego (Daniel 3:19-23). I couldn't imagine walking into that!

I used to play with candles in the basement. I liked fire. I think most kids do. I'd light the candle and let the wax drip in my hands. If I held the burning candle just right, the wax would drip evenly and make little circles. I used to pretend I was doing that commercial for corn removal. I would let the wax drip and harden, and then I'd say, "Drop on Freeze-on, lift off corn!" Once the wax had become hard, you could pick if off easily and in one piece. It worked perfectly.

One time I was playing with the candle and doing the commercial thing when Moma called me from upstairs. I put out the candle (or so I thought) and went to see what Moma wanted. Well, a short time later someone smelled smoke. You see, we had a lot of stuff in the basement: towels, blankets, my father's old clothes, etc. I guess when I put out the candle I let it drop on this pile of stuff. I thought I had blown the candle completely out, but apparently not. Moma ran downstairs and saved the day. She put the fire out before it did too much damage. I was so scared. I'm sure I denied having anything to do with that fire. I don't think I got a whuppin', but everyone suspected me. That was the last time I played the *Drop on Freeze-on, lift off corn* game.

Sometimes I would go down into the basement and pretend I was in a haunted house. I would be real quiet and listen to all the sounds coming from upstairs. I would be able to hear voices and footsteps. And since we had windows downstairs, I could look outside and see the shadows from the trees blowing in the wind. Every now and then, a stray cat or dog would pass by the window. These were wild animals stalking prey (little girls alone in the basement) in the night. I could scare myself to death!

Once, while playing out my Vincent Price fantasies, nobody knew I was downstairs and they turned the lights off on me. It was pitch black. I ran up the stairs screaming and trying to open the basement door. To my surprise it was locked! I was trapped. I was sure something was following me up the stairs, and there I stood with no place to go. I yelled and screamed and cried until someone opened the door. It was Moma. She asked me what in the world I was doing in the basement. Then she demanded to know who turned the lights off on me.

That basement was my haven. I had so much fun down there. But, later on, after I was grown, I went back home and *had* to go down to the basement. It was musty, dirty, and probably had rats and other critters living there. And there was so much junk. It was truly a fire hazard. I couldn't imagine *wanting* to be down there. I couldn't imagine what I thought was so much fun.

Piano Lessons

I remember in the second or third grade, we got to pick out an instrument that we wanted to learn to play. I picked the violin. I took it home that night and promptly returned it the next day. I wanted nothing to do with it. How could people possibly keep that thing under their chin? It was just too much trouble.

That's when I decided I wanted to play the piano. Maybe it was because one of my sisters played the piano. But then my brother played the trumpet (as well as other instruments), and my oldest sister played the clarinet. Well, the piano it was.

Now, Moma wasn't having this "learn to play by rote" stuff. I had to take piano lessons and learn how to read music. Oh, brother! It wasn't my idea to be a concert pianist; I just wanted to learn how to play. No matter, cuz' soon thereafter I started with the lessons.

My first piano lessons were with this family that lived way out. It seemed as though they had an orchard or a farm or something. I can clearly remember Moma driving up into their long, crowded driveway. They always had several cars and sometimes trucks. They had beautiful flowers and lots of things growing on their property. There were these twins, Charlene and Marlene. One of them gave me my piano lessons. I think my sister took lessons from them also, but not at the same time as mine.

These people were so nice. They had a lovely house with what looked like a new piano. Our piano was old and big. Some of the keys would stick. So when you played certain notes, you had to lift up the key real fast before you had to hit it again. Otherwise, it would remain stuck and there went your masterpiece. My sister and I got good at unsticking the keys as we went. Pretty soon it was second nature to us.

I think I took my lessons on Saturday mornings. One of the twins would always be there to greet me and Moma. My lesson probably lasted about an hour. I would play hymns and classical music.

Sometimes, when I didn't practice like I was supposed to, I would start off playing the songs real well. My teacher would start singing along as accompaniment. Everything would be fine 'til I got to the harder parts. Since I hadn't practiced, I couldn't keep up the correct pace of the song. I played faster on the easy parts and slower (missing several notes) on the hard parts. That kind of playing makes singing along very difficult. I would be so embarrassed. She knew I hadn't practiced like I should have. But she was so gracious and told me how important it was to keep up the tempo throughout the entire song. She told me how important it was to practice. She told me I had potential and that she knew I could be good if I wanted to. I would always promise to practice and do better next week.

I used to have to put little figurines on the top of my hands while I was playing (I think they were plastic soldiers). This was to make sure my hands were in the correct playing position. If they stayed on, that meant my hand posture was good. If they fell off, ooops! It didn't take me long to get the hang of it. After too many times of having to stop, pick up those bad boys, and start over again…well, let's just say it wasn't the highlight of my practice session.

As soon as I got home from my piano lesson I would practice. Moma's favorite song was *Amazing Grace*. She loved to hear me play that song. She'd say, "Baby, play that song for me. You play so well." I would always oblige, although sometimes begrudgingly. Other times, I would be playing *Green Onions* by Booker T. and the MGs (a song which I taught myself by listening to the record) or *Peter Gunn*. Those were cool songs. I'd always add another octave, lower of course, which gave it a much richer tone.

When I was older, I started taking lessons from this older lady who lived on Sixth Street. Her name was Mrs. Braves. She used to make me sing with my piano lessons. She would have me practice my breathing techniques as well. I used to think, "Now what does this have to do with playing the piano?" I would have to stand against the wall, tall and straight, and breathe in and out. She would tell me not to breathe with my chest and shoulders, but from my diaphragm. The whole time she would have her fingers in my diaphragm so she could tell whether or not I was doing it correctly. Sometimes she would push so hard it would hurt. How could I possibly breathe with her fingers punching in my ribs?

Then she would tell me to watch the "Lawrence Welk Show." Apparently, on that show they had terrific singers that could help me learn. But I had to draw the line, okay?

This one time I was at Mrs. Braves' house taking lessons when she was cooking. She usually cooked vegetables, as she was pretty healthy. Apparently, she was steaming them when all of a sudden the top blew off. The noise was so blunt, sharp, and unexpected that it really scared me. I didn't know if somebody was shooting at us, or what. Those vegetables started flying all over the house. My sister must have had her lesson right after mine cuz' she witnessed the whole thing. Carrots, celery, potatoes, and turnips were all over the floor. Mrs. Braves kept saying, "Oh, my." My sister and I still laugh about that.

You know, I think I breathe correctly today thanks to Mrs. Braves. I breathe from my diaphragm and not my chest area. I never get short winded, and I have good posture, too. And even though on cable they show reruns, I still won't watch the "Lawrence Welk Show."

THE BLACKS

I remember our next door neighbors, the Blacks. They were an older couple with two sons. They had the most beautiful flowers growing in their yard. There were enormous, tropical-looking flowers with large blooms of white, pink, yellow, and red. I used to sit in the front yard and spend hours just looking at them. They put me in sort of a trance.

Along with the beautiful flowers, the Blacks had fruit trees. Not just any fruit trees, but the good kind. They had cherry trees, apple trees, and I think pear trees. Everyone used to come and steal the cherries from their cherry tree in the back yard. But not me. I always asked first. I didn't want to get caught and told on. You see, Mr. Black was kind of scary.

Mr. Black drank a lot. And he was a fast talking man. I often thought he was from Jamaica or somewhere cuz' he had this accent (or maybe he was talking so fast I just couldn't tell what he was saying). His wife was a large woman who moved and spoke very slowly. She had a whinny, singsong voice. Mrs. Black was a church-going woman. On Sundays she would be all dressed up in her white. Sundays also meant fried chicken. This woman made the best fried chicken I've ever tasted. It was seasoned just right. I loved the drumsticks and the wings the best.

Mr. and Mrs. Black were always fighting. I'm not sure if they ever fought physically, but he was always cussing at her. She would be saying, "Oh, Tomey (I think his name was Tommie, but with the whine in her voice it sounded like Tomey), you shouldn't talk like that." Now understand that one little sentence would take her about three minutes to say because she spoke so slowly. She would draw out every syllable to the max. To this, Mr. Black would respond, "Shut up woman. Don't no one want to hear your shit!" This sentence took Mr. Black about three nanoseconds to say. If I hadn't been so scared, it would have been funny listening to their exchange.

On many occasions, Mr. Black would just get in his car and leave the house. He always parked in the back and drove down the alley. Mrs. Black would be saying, "Tomey, don't you leave this house. I coming with you." To this Mr. Black would respond, "By the time you get out of that house woman, I'll be in Seattle" (Seattle was 144 miles away!).

I remember many a night laying in bed with Moma and hearing the Blacks fight. Her bedroom window was on the side of the house closest to the Black's yard. I would be so afraid. I would pray to God that they would stop fighting and that no one would get hurt. You see, I experienced a lot of physical abuse. Of course, none of it was ever aimed directly at me, but it may as well have been. I took it all very personally. I cried and felt every harsh word and every punch that was thrown as if they we meant for me. I felt abused. I couldn't understand why people had to act that way. What was wrong with them?

One night, Mr. Black went on one of his drunken rampages. I remember distinctly, because I was in the bathroom and could hear them fighting through the open window. I was probably sitting on the toilet praying. Next thing I know, Moma is banging on the bathroom door telling me to come out. Now, I'm sitting there minding my own business (and trying to take care of business!). Didn't she know what I was doing? I just couldn't come out. And, what did she want anyway? I was busy. But, there was this urgency in her voice, and I knew better than to try and ignore her demand. So, I tried to clean myself as best I could in such a hurry and came out muttering to myself, "This better be good."

Well, come to find out Mr. Black had hit his oldest son in the head with a jar of pickles, dill pickles to be exact. They were the good kind, too, big and juicy. His son's head was bleeding really bad. I don't remember much after that. I'm sure he had to be taken to the hospital cuz' he was bleeding all over the place (Yuk! What a mess). Moma wrapped a towel around his head to stop the bleeding. I was so scared. I kept wondering, "Why did he hit him with the pickles?" This episode gave a whole new meaning to the phrase *food fight*!

The next day I remember wondering to myself if this had really happened or if it was all a bad dream. But, as I passed by the Black's house I could see big, green, dill pickles lying all over the front yard. It was like spotting Easter eggs hidden amongst the grass. I used to love those pickles and kept thinking to myself, "I wonder if they're still good"…

The Mills

I remember the neighbors that lived across the street, the Mills. This family was quite large. So large, I'm not sure that anybody knew exactly how many there were.

Mr. and Mrs. Mills were like the patriarch and matriarch of the clan. I think they were of Indian decent, which is not surprising since Yakima, Washington is Indian country. Rumor had it that they were sort of like an Indian Mafia. You know, drugs, prostitution, gambling, etc.

During the summertime there would be any number of kids outside playing in their yard. Their yard, however, didn't have any grass. I wondered if it was because of all those kids stomping around. They reminded me of a colony of ants. You couldn't count how many there were, but you knew there were a lot. I used to play with them every day. There was Robbie and Bobbie (I think they were uncle and nephew even though they were very close in age), Sidney (their cousin), Jeanie, Sandy, Veronica, and Lulu (sisters) just to name a few. They would come over and play in our back yard too.

Our back yard had all kinds of good stuff to eat. We had peach trees, apricot trees, grapes, strawberries, blackberries, and raspberries. We also had a garden. There were turnips, cucumbers, tomatoes, beans, and all kinds of other healthy stuff. I used to pick the cucumbers and turnips, wash them, put salt on them, and eat them raw. Our next door neighbors, the Blacks, had apple trees and cherry trees. That was the life.

There were grown Mills' children, too. Two of the older girls, Laurie and Shelley, were my sisters' ages. I think Laurie was into drugs and prostitution.

She was real skinny, and some of her teeth were missing. Sometimes, men in cars would approach us and ask us if we wanted a ride. Well, we knew what that meant. Moma always told us when that happened to just keep our heads high, look straight ahead, and say, "No thank you." She knew what was going on, and she knew how to get us out of that predicament with respect. She told us to just keep on steppin'. And we did.

One night Laurie came over really late. It was dark outside. Apparently, she had forgotten her key to the house and couldn't get in. She wanted me to climb through a window and unlock the front door. To my surprise, my mother said okay. Had she lost her mind? I would have to go around to the back of their yard, stand on top of a box, and climb through a back window. It was no telling what was lurking around in their back yard at night. I looked at my mother very carefully with my head cocked and my eyes slanted as if looking through the eye of a needle. I was hoping this would let her know I did not approve of her decision. Why was she picking now, of all times, to be a good neighbor? Had she forgotten who these people were? I mean playing with them during the daylight hours was one thing, but going in their back yard alone with the drug-addict prostitute late at night was a whole different story.

I was so scared, and Laurie knew it. She kept telling me not to be afraid because there was nothing in their back yard. Yeah right, I thought. Easy for you to say. No telling what you've been doing. Whatever it was, I'm sure it was scarier than going in your back yard at night. I remember walking very deliberately and looking at every square inch of the ground as if we were walking in a minefield. I could hear every piece of dirt I stepped on. It would go "squish" and "crunch" underneath my feet. Were we in a jungle? Was I going to see the eyes of a tiger staring at me through the bushes? Was a lion going to jump me when I had my head turned the other way? Was a big bear going to eat me? Were there snakes slithering on the ground? Lordy, I just knew I was going to die, and Laurie sure wasn't going to be of any help. She didn't even have her key! How could Moma do this to me? I thought she loved me.

After we walked what seemed like an hour, we finally reached the back yard. Laurie kept telling me what to do: move the box underneath the window, stand on it, but keep steady or you'll fall. I thought to myself, if you know so much then you do it. Well I got the window open, crawled through and opened the door for Laurie. She started hugging and kissing me and saying, "Thank you so much." Thank you, what? Where was the money? Did she think I was doing this for free? After all, I had risked my life walking through that jungle with all of those wild animals.

Just then, I heard this voice saying, "Laurie is that you? Where you been girl?" Who was that? I thought nobody was home. I ran out that door so fast that I'm sure Laurie only saw the soles of my feet. I got into our house, slammed and locked both the screen door and the front door. I was huffing and puffing so loud, Moma asked me if I was all right. I could see her laughing. She thought it was funny.

After I realized I was safe, I thought it was funny too. Moma hugged me and let me have some ice cream. The safari in the Mills' back yard was worth it after all.

Miss Alice

I remember one of my mother's best friends, Miss Alice. We called her "Miss" Alice because it was neither proper nor polite to call a grown-up by their first name alone. It didn't seem right to call her by her full name (first and last), so we put Miss in front of her first name and that was acceptable as respectable. I don't think we addressed anyone else in that manner. But, then we didn't know anyone else like Miss Alice.

Miss Alice was always cool, calm, and collected. She was so much fun. She and my mother were friends for years and years. I used to play with one of her younger daughters. We were best friends too. My mother used to sew dresses for us out of the same material and pattern. We would look like sisters. Come to think of it, she even had the same first name as my sister.

Whenever we got in trouble, or if Moma was in a bad mood, we would call up Miss Alice on the phone and beg her to come over. We'd say, "Please come over, Miss Alice. Moma is on the rampage and we need help." She'd come over and calm Moma down every time. She'd say, "Now Frances, don't be so hard on those kids. Those are good kids." In the meantime, we'd be standing in a corner listening like hostages, waiting and watching in anticipation while the bomb squad dismantled some deadly explosives. Then we'd say, "Oh thank you, Miss Alice. We don't know what we'd do without you." She would just laugh and say she understood.

Miss Alice used to smoke cigarettes. Not just any cigarettes, Camels. Those bad boys were the strongest on the market. One time I picked up one of her butts from the ashtray and took a puff. Of course, she had put it out completely, so I was smoking a dead butt. When I inhaled, I thought I was going to die. I started choking, and the tears came pouring out of my eyes. My lungs were burning, and I couldn't breathe. I thought to myself, how in the world can she smoke these things? But she did, and one after another. This experience gave me a whole new respect for that woman.

Miss Alice and my mother (and others) used to play cards all the time. They would play Bid Whist. We would stand around for hours watching them. They would be laughing and talking and playing for hours on end. Moma would be drinking Tab, or some other diet drink, and Miss Alice would be drinking Coca-Cola and smoking Camels. Those were joyous memories. Everyone was happy whether they were winning or losing. I used to go around the table and look in everyone's hands. I felt so privileged knowing who held what cards.

Moma and Miss Alice used to walk to the park all the time. They would go shopping together and take turns visiting each other too. They talked about everything. They were the epitome of friendship. I considered Miss Alice my second mother. That's how close we were. I'd go to her house to visit, and she'd always say, "Come on in, Vetress. The door is open, baby."

Even after I became an adult and moved away, I'd go back home to visit and would always go see Miss Alice. I would sit there and talk to her for hours. I'm sure she and my mother are in heaven right now talking up a storm. "Oh, Alice, blah, blah, blah. Frances, you need to stop, girl"…

My Sister's Boyfriend

I remember my sister having lots of boyfriends. She was smart, witty, and very good looking. I was always so envious of her. There was this one guy that I'll never forget. I think that's because he was so much in love with her. He would have done anything for my sister, and he did (she saw to it!).

This guy was just a little taller than she. He was bow-legged, very soft-spoken, and had a nice smile. He dressed well and had a great car. I think he drove a bronze-like colored Chevrolet which he kept spotless (my sister wasn't about to ride in a car that was anything less than impeccable!). He used to let her drive all the time, and of course, I got to go for rides.

She was quite demanding of this particular boyfriend. She had him doing all sorts of stuff, just because he would. I'm not sure he ever put his foot down, and if he did, she could always talk him into doing whatever she wanted. She used to make him go and get us hamburgers and french fries all the time. I don't remember what kind of job he had, but it must have paid well cuz' he spent money on her like she was a queen.

One time when he came over to visit, I noticed this big bulge in his pants. It caught my eye because of the size and shape. It looked as if he had something in his pocket, something big and slightly slanted. I studied it for awhile trying to guess what it was. It couldn't be a pencil, although the shape was right, it was too big. It could have been the handle of a screwdriver, but what would he be doing with that in his pants? Besides, that would have been dangerous. He could have hurt himself if it had stuck him. I know he saw me looking. He was probably wishing that I would just disappear. NO WAY!

This bulge was bugging me so much that I finally got up the nerve to ask him about it. As I recall, there were other people in the room when I blurted out pointing, "Hey, what's that in your pocket?" Without even looking down, he quickly answered, "Nothing." Well, I wasn't about to let it rest, cuz' it was obvious that something was there, and I wanted to know what it was. So, I asked again in an insisting tone. I said to him, "Yes, there is something in your pocket. It's right there, see?" I tried to touch it so he would realize that something really was there. It was not my imagination working overtime. He caught my hand before I could get a grip on this "bulge." Laughing nervously, he said to me again that nothing was in his pocket. Now I may have been young, but I wasn't stupid. I could clearly see even though I did wear glasses. Why was he denying the fact that something was there? Why didn't he want to tell me what it was? The more he denied it, the more I insisted on knowing what it was.

The room got very quiet. I kept looking at this thing making the odd shape in his pants. I really wanted to touch it thinking that way maybe I could figure out what it was by feeling it. But, he wouldn't let me get near him. He was acting so strange. What was the big secret? Why wasn't anyone saying anything? Didn't they realize that if they had just told me what it was, that I would go away? This whole ordeal could be settled in a matter of seconds with one quick answer. Surely everyone could see it. And by the look on their faces, they knew what it was.

I'm not sure what happened next. I think he probably gave me a large sum of money to go away. I don't think the subject ever came up again. But I've figured out what that bulge was. O-o-o-h-h-h...

KEMPER'S

I remember when my father used to work at Kemper's. Kemper's was a hamburger stand located not too far from our house. He would clean up there at night.

Sometimes, we would all go with him and help him clean. I'm not sure if anyone got paid (I know I didn't), but we got to eat hamburgers and bring home ice cream. On several occasions, I would sneak candy bars too.

We used to have to get up like at 1:00 or 2:00 in the morning to go there. It would usually take three to four hours to clean the whole place so it was ready for business the next day. Sometimes, when I was sleeping in Moma's bed and it was time to get up, I would wave my hand for them to go away and say, "I'm too tired to go to work." But, when they came home with the treats, I'd be mad that I didn't go with them. I'd tell them to *make* me go with next time, no matter what I said.

When I did go, I'd sweep the outside parking lot in front and back with one of those big brooms that had the long handle. Those kinds of brooms had bristles that were wide so it looked like somebody grinning real big. My father was very picky about how you cleaned, so I had to do it right, getting up all of the dirt, paper, and cigarette butts. It was hard work. I'd often stop sweeping when cars would pass by to see if I knew the people inside. I would wonder where they were going at that time of night.

My father usually cleaned the wooden mats that were inside himself. There would be at least six or seven sets of those things. Each set had about ten individual pieces of wood tied together with rope. He would take each set outside and wash them thoroughly on his hands and knees with a brush and bucket. My older sisters used to tell him to use the broom with soap and water. This way, the mats would still be clean, and it wouldn't be so hard on his back. But, he wouldn't do it that way.

My sisters mopped the floor and cleaned the grills. They would have to scrape off all of the leftover hamburger drippings and grease before scrubbing the grills with a brillo pad. Those grills would be shining when my sisters got through cleaning them. I would be impressed. They didn't clean our house that good.

There were a lot of those big garbage cans outside that had to be emptied and cleaned. They were the two-piece kind where the top came off. They were too heavy for me to lift, but I could get the tops off. I think they had plastic bags lined on the inside and someone would have to carefully take those out, tie them up, and dispose of them without spilling trash all over the place. This process required gloves cuz' you didn't want to be touching the stuff that was in them with your bare hands. It would be all smelly and sometimes there would be ants and flies too.

On more than one occasion, my father would have to go directly to his other job straight from Kemper's. When this happened, we would have to walk home. By this time though, it would be daylight, and since we'd be looking dirty and tired after cleaning, we didn't want anyone to see us. My sisters used to run and leave me behind. They knew I couldn't keep up. They thought that was so funny. But I didn't care, especially if I knew I had ice cream I could eat later. We would get the marble kind, strawberry, chocolate, and vanilla. Sometime, we got ice cream sandwiches too. I don't think my father knew we took as much stuff as we did. He would not have approved.

We worked hard back then. But we certainly knew how to get our due pay, even if it was food instead of dollars.

CONVERSATIONS WITH THE DEVIL

I remember sleeping in the bedroom with the bunk beds. They were situated right next to the window. I could see the hedges and the empty field outside the window. We used to play baseball in that field. Although there was dirt, weeds, rocks, and sometimes broken glass (which I used to pretend was precious gems glittering in all of its splendor) it served well as a baseball diamond. I'm surprised that nobody ever got seriously hurt.

On several occasions I would have this dream where I would be in the bunk bed looking out of the window. All of a sudden the devil would appear. He would be standing right outside the window with his black cape lined in red satin and horns sticking out of the side of his head. His pitchfork would be by his side and yes, he had the long black tail. I don't remember this devil being of any specific ethnic background, though. He was just *The Devil*.

Now, please understand that I wasn't afraid, nor was the devil threatening me. We would be engaged in these conversations. I can't tell you what we were talking about. No, not because it was a secret, I just can't remember! There was no screaming or violence. There were no raised voices. There was just conversation, much like chatting with the next door neighbor.

Maybe I had been watching too many cartoons. Maybe the theme in church revolved around Revelations. I'm not sure what these conversations with the devil were all about. I do remember, however, having many similar conversations with my father. We would talk for hours about various subjects. To be honest, these talks would be more like debates. I would take the position of, "just because its written in black and white doesn't make it true. You shouldn't believe everything you read." Then there was something about Nikita Kruschev and Russia. What was that? Was he just humoring me by letting me talk on and on? I thought I was so smart then. Whenever my sisters would overhear our conversations, they would comment on how I seemed to be able to hold my own with my father.

Now, these conversations with my father, as with the devil, would be very frustrating. He was always calm, taking a position I really didn't understand. But it was always opposite mine. I felt as if I was trying to teach him something but that he wasn't getting it, or rather didn't want to get it. I would be so serious using examples to get my point across. He would just sit there reciting some verbiage that really had no relevance to the subject. It was like talking to a Chatty Cathy doll. I guess that's the price you pay when no one else will play with you.

This dream with the devil was recurring. It seemed so real. It's as if when I went to sleep at night I knew he would reappear. Didn't he have anything better to do than to bug me at night? Maybe no one would play with him either.

When you're lonely and have an active imagination, you can come up with all sorts of stuff. I guess that's why Boley was created…

Boley

I remember having this imaginary friend named Boley. I'm not sure where Boley came from or how this friend came to be known as Boley. I don't even know if Boley was a girl or a boy. Sometimes imaginary friends aren't of a specific gender or ethnicity. The important thing is that they are friends with whom you can share your inner most secrets without fear or embarrassment.

My first memory of the two of us was sitting on the front porch talking. The front door was open, but the screen door was shut (to keep out the flies or me, as my sisters would tell it). Boley and I were having a good time. We were whispering and giggling and saying things that only best friends could share. What I didn't know was that one of my sisters was standing inside the screen door listening and watching. After a while she just couldn't stand it anymore. She burst out in laughter and asked me who in the world I was talking to. I looked up in surprise. You'd think I'd just seen a ghost. My eyes got as big as plates, and my mouth dropped wide open. She couldn't know anything about Boley. Boley was my friend. I was horrified that she heard us, and even worse that she would tell somebody. I tried to hide Boley by pushing my friend behind me. What was I going to do? How was I going to explain this?

She ran laughing into the kitchen telling my other sister that I was outside talking to Boley. She was in hysterics tying to describe what she had just witnessed. I ran in after her trying to defend myself (and my friend). I began to stammer and stutter as I desperately offered some lame-brained explanation of what was going on. At first, my other sister didn't quite know what to make of the conversation. She just looked at me with her hands on her hips, her eyebrows furrowed, and her lips pursed closely together. I felt my face getting hot. My eyes were burning with the tears I fought back. I could feel them streaming down my cheeks. I was being mocked once again. I was being betrayed. You see this is the very reason I had an imaginary friend. My sisters didn't understand. They simply could not be trusted with my feelings.

Later on in the day all I heard was, "Dee Dee, where's Boley? Did Boley get tired of playing with you? Did Boley have to go home?" They thought they were so funny. I was thoroughly humiliated. I refused to discuss Boley with them. It was none of their business. They didn't know anything about Boley, and I wasn't going to tell them. As far as I was concerned, they never had to play with me again. I had a true friend.

Boley and I made mud pies together, we played in the back yard together, and we read books together. We even watched cartoons together! Whenever I said my prayers, I included words of encouragement for Boley. I was so happy that I had a friend of my own.

Boley and I were best friends for what seemed like forever. I don't remember what happened to Boley or when. One day, Boley just ceased to exist. I don't remember being sad or crying. It was if I realized that it was time for Boley to leave. There wasn't a going away party or any big announcement, but Boley was gone.

I remember watching a *Twilight Zone* episode where the main character's name was Boley. This Boley was a boxer, who was involved in a racket where he would illegally win his fights. Well this little boy really believed in Boley, and thought he was the best boxer that ever lived. A time came when Boley was on his own and had to fight for real. He knew he wasn't going to win and that the scam would be over. He was ashamed and felt badly that the little boy thought he was so good. The little boy kept saying, "Boley, you can do it. You gotta' believe. You gotta' believe, Boley." Needless to say, Boley lost the fight and his honor as well. He lost everything because he didn't believe. If you *really* believe and have faith, you can accomplish anything!

I'll never forget Boley (my Boley). You never forget your best friends no matter how long ago they were a part of your life. To this day my sisters still remember Boley and how important my friend was to me. Only now they don't tease me. They speak of Boley with sincere emotions and not ridicule. Goodnight Boley, wherever you are.

A Heavenly Dream

I remember all of my dreams, and I dream in living color. I've been told this is very unusual. It seems perfectly natural to me since this has always been the case.

One night I had a dream about heaven. Now, getting to this place was no easy task. But, once I made it there, the view and the feeling of accomplishment was absolutely incredible! I started out on what seemed to be a strenuous hike. Now that I think about it, that hike reminded me of the time I climbed Mount Sinai (I thought I was going to die!).

The path was straight up with lots of unsteady rocks and cliffs. There were others with me, however, I cannot recall if I knew them. I know one thing—these other people were not helping me. I can remember slipping and sliding and almost falling into what must have been oblivion. I was so far up that I could not see the ground. And there was no turning back. How did I get here? What on earth (or in the name of heaven) was I doing and why?

The trek went on forever (at least that's the only dream I remember having that night). I had scrapes and scratches all over my body. There were thistles and jagged rocks all over the place. I remember tree branches growing out of the rocks. These branches, on more than one occasion, saved me from falling into the abyss. I had to rest frequently. Perhaps it was the altitude, or maybe I was just out of shape. I was huffing and puffing and gasping for breath. I was so tired, but I couldn't be left behind. I had to keep up.

I remember seeing huge clouds and sometimes blue skies. It reminded me of cartoons when the bald eagle would fly so high that he could see everything below. Sometimes the wind would blow very hard, and the rain would soak all of my clothing (I don't remember wearing appropriate hiking clothes or boots either. Nope, no Eddie Bauer!). I remember being very afraid yet determined to finish the hike. It was though I knew something spectacular would be waiting. And, strangely enough, I felt as though I wasn't alone (no, I'm not talking about the other hikers! If you will recall, they were not interested in coming to my aid. Now, is that any way to act on the way to heaven?).

After what felt like an eternity, I stopped. In looking around I was in awe. I had never seen such a site (even in my dreams). It was beautiful beyond words, an inexplicable beauty. Everything was so clear and bright. I was higher than the highest high. The colors were magnificent. I saw mountains and hills. I saw valleys. I saw endless blue skies and clouds that looked whiter than new fallen snow. The clouds were gigantic billowing masses. I was full of energy and happiness, no anxiety nor worries. This had to be heaven. But, there was no singing, and I didn't see any angels. I didn't see any streets of gold (or gravel either for that matter). But I knew that there was no place like this on earth. I wasn't alone, yet I don't remember seeing any other people. The scrapes and scratches were no longer visible. I'm not even sure if my body was still in its previous state. All I knew was I was experiencing something so incredible that I could not speak.

I remember awaking and feeling like I had just experienced the ultimate sensation. I sat up in my bed and wondered what had just happened. Was I still in my house? What had just taken place? Why was my heart racing? I could still feel the wonder and amazement of heaven. It was truly extraordinary. I knew that I never wanted that feeling to leave me. I wanted to go back. I was in ecstasy. I wanted to tell somebody. I wanted to tell everybody. But I couldn't explain it, although I could still see and feel it.

I've never had another dream like that. If you have that dream once, you don't need to have it ever again. I'll never forget the hard road to heaven and the reward of getting there. I feel blessed to have had the experience.

The Holiness Church

I remember there was a church right around the corner from where we lived. Although we didn't belong to this particular church, we knew most of the members that did. As a matter of fact, we went to school with some of them.

When they would have services at night, we could open our bedroom window and hear the singing and shouting. It sounded like there were hundreds of people in attendance when in reality there would only be a few. Sometimes we would walk around the corner, park ourselves on the people's grass that lived across the street from the church, listen, and watch. The door to this church would always be open so we could see everything that went on. It was better than going to the movies. We got a first hand view of all the action. And let me tell you, there was plenty of action.

It would be in the summertime when we watched from across the street. Late at night, the temperature would be in the 70s if not the 80s. So, it behooved them to leave the door of the church open, otherwise, there would be no ventilation (unless you counted the jumping, shouting, speaking in tongues, and crying). We would sit there for hours and hours.

From where we sat we had a birdseye view of the center isle and both sides of the church where there were rows of pews. If we timed it just right, we could get there just as all the action was heating up. They had a piano that somebody was playing like nobody's business and a choir that was literally rocking the house. It seemed as though we could see the walls vibrating and feel the heat that was being generated. We would be clapping our hands and tapping our feet on that lawn. We would even sing along, though I don't know how we did that since we didn't know the words.

Pretty soon, the shouting would begin. Everyone inside would be dancing around with their hands in the air. They would have a beat going that was unmistakably gospel. I mean down-home, foot stomping, hand clapping, head bobbing, gospel! There would be harmonizing, solos, laughing, crying, shouting, people rolling on the floor and praising God to the highest heavens. You could hear these people for blocks.

One time our church got invited there for a special service. We were supposed to participate in the program, and then this church would reciprocate. Well, somebody from our church didn't show up. Everyone was looking around to see what was going to happen. Then Moma stands up and says that I can play the piano and sing. What?! Had she become delirious? Had the heat gotten to her? I wasn't about to get up in front of that church, play the piano, and sing. If I had known I was going to be part of the entertainment, I would have come down with a fever and had to stay home. At first, I protested quietly in her ear. But she wasn't having that. Then I told her that I needed my music to play the piano (which of course, I didn't have with me). She said no problem. Since we only lived around the corner, one of my sisters could run home, get it, and be back in seconds. I thought, Oh Lord. What am I going to do?

Like a big baby, I started crying. Moma didn't care. I was going to sing and play if it took all night. She was so proud of me, and all I did was protest. I felt like dying. I knew some of the people in that church. What would they think? Their songs were hopping. My playing and singing was like eating plain rice with no milk and sugar in comparison. I was so embarrassed. I got up, played my little song and sang, crying through the whole thing. It seemed like I was up there forever. I couldn't even see the expressions on any of the faces because of the tears in my eyes. My voice was quivering and heaving like an angry sea during a violent storm because I was crying so hard. Imagine, someone singing and crying their heart out at the same time. Well, that was me.

Finally, it was over. Moma stood up and clapped for me because I had represented our church. Oh, brother! Everyone told me I did a good job. But I knew better. I must have sounded like a drowning rat caught in a mousetrap. Yes, I was feeling that much frustration and pain. Probably not nearly the amount of pain the people listening were feeling. I was sure I could hear dogs howling outside. If I had been in a cartoon strip, I would have been the cat on the fence getting the boots thrown at him. I was sure that I was the laughing stock of the town. I was sure that I'd never live it down. Somehow, I made it, though. God is with you…even through the stupid stuff.

Mr. Thinn

I remember when I was in the fifth grade I had this teacher named Mr. Thinn. Mr. Thinn actually was quite slender and most of his head was bald (although he did have a little hair on the sides and back). The thing I remember most about Mr. Thinn was when he got mad, which he did often, his face and the top part of his bald head would turn bright red!

Mr. Thinn was a good teacher. A lot of the kids thought he was mean. If your desk was messy, he would make you stay after school and clean it up. One time, he was yelling at one of the students, and they were both standing in the doorway. I thought to myself, "Boy, I sure hate to have to pass them. He'll probably find something to yell at me about." Thinking this, I decided to pass quietly without making any kind of eye contact. Well, he starts yelling at me, "Don't be so rude. Don't you know how to say excuse me?" I was so mad at him. I wanted to say, "If you weren't so mean, you wouldn't be standing here in the middle of the doorway yelling at somebody!" Of course, instead I mumbled a feeble "excuse me" and rushed by them both.

I think he must have had high blood pressure or something and that's why he got so red. I often had conversations with other students about why he yelled so much. What was he so mad about all of the time? Did he dislike us that much? We weren't that bad. We wondered if he yelled at his wife that way. We wondered if he even had a wife. Who would want to be married to a meanie like him?

Outside of our classroom there was a cement sidewalk. And right next to that there were tetherball poles. We'd play there at recess. Our classroom was the next to the last one on that side of the building. So, if you were walking to the auditorium or to the principal's office, you had a long haul. Mr. Thinn would walk very fast with his arms swinging like everything was of utmost urgency. He swung his arms like he was in the Russian army, and he got to that auditorium in no time flat. His face would be all red, but he got there before anybody else.

I remember one time we were eating lunch. I had bought my lunch that day, and we had some really nasty-tasting vegetables. I thought I was being so sneaky and stuffed the vegetables in my milk carton. I folded the milk carton, put my tray up, and then threw everything in the trash (including the milk carton with the nasty vegetables inside). That mission was accomplished and I could go outside and play tetherball. Well, apparently Mr. Thinn had seen me (and I thought I was being so careful). He made me take the milk carton out of the garbage and eat those vegetables! I was so hurt that I started crying. How could he do this to me? I was a good student. I just didn't want to eat those nasty-tasting vegetables. It took me awhile, but I finally got them all down. I was the last one in the room, though. But before I went out to recess (which was almost over because it had taken me so long to eat those vegetables), and much to my surprise, he came up to me and put some caramels in my hand. He said, "Shhhh – don't tell anyone." I couldn't believe it! What was he doing with caramels? Mean, old Mr. Thinn was actually doing something nice. I didn't know what to say. Then, thank you came to mind cuz' I knew I had better say something. I went outside and won every game of tetherball I played.

There was an intercom in all of the rooms, which was connected to a public announcement system. At the time, I was in the school play and was supposed to be in the auditorium for an afternoon practice. I was one of the narrators because my voice carried so well (I had a big mouth and everyone could hear me!). I guess I had forgotten and was sitting there quietly doing my work. All of a sudden, Mr. Thinn's voice came across the PA system, saying, "Vee-tress, are you coming to the auditorium? We can't start without you." Everybody turned around and looked at me. I froze and didn't know what to say. Again, I hear his voice, "Vetress, get down here right now!" Someone said for me, "She's on her way, Mr. Thinn." I got up and ran to that auditorium. I think I broke his record that day!

    I must have been in junior high or high school when I heard that Mr. Thinn had passed away. Someone told me he had a heart attack. They believed he had high blood pressure. I felt so sad. All I could remember was those caramels he had given me that day. He really wasn't so mean.

My First Period

I remember when I first started menstruating. Now, Moma had prepared me for this, and we had seen the films in school, too. But somehow when it actually happened, it was a whole different story.

One night, everyone was in the living room. There was a card table in the middle of the room, and we were either playing cards or dominoes. There was a rocking chair behind the card table, a big chair underneath the picture window (with a doily that Moma had crocheted), and a couch along the side of the wall. Hmmm, I guess that was kinda like a family night (I didn't think we had that!).

Anyway, I go to the bathroom, pull down my panties, sit on the toilet, and look down. That's when I saw it…blood! It was a deep red (quite a pretty color, actually) and covered the better part of my panty crotch. Oh, my Lord, I was menstruating. Why did this have to happen to me now? Was I old enough? What was I going to do?

I sat there for awhile contemplating my next move. I told myself not to panic. I told myself that I wasn't the first person who started her period. Then it hit me. Just go tell Moma. She'll know what to do and she'll be discreet. Well, how was I going to do this with everyone in the living room? I didn't want everyone to know. I didn't want anyone to know (except Moma, she had to know!).

I went into the living room and whispered into Moma's ear. She looked at me and said, "Don't worry, I'll help you." She got me some santi-panties and a sanitary napkin. Now, these santi-panties had a plastic lining (to prevent leaks) and two hook-like gadgets sewn in at both ends of the crotch. The idea was to pull the ends of the sanitary napkin through the two hook-like gadgets so it would be secure and stay in place. At that time, the sanitary napkins were so big and bulky (it felt like you had a big, ol' pillow between your legs!) that it would take a small miracle to hold the thing in place. The padding was so thick that if you bled that much surely you would be in need of a blood transfusion. And, tampons? Oh, no. You could forget using those.

After we got everything squared away, I returned into the living room. All eyes were on me. But, I didn't get it. My sisters kept asking me how I felt. I wasn't sick, so why were they asking me that? Oh, brother, they knew! Did Moma tell them? How could she do that? Did they hear me whispering in her ear? If I could have turned red, I would have. What an ordeal.

Little did I know that the ordeal was just beginning. How was I going to deal with this situation in school? I was probably the only one that had started menstruating. They didn't make those nice little purse-like pouches to carry the napkins in. And, they were so big that it was hard to hide them. To top it all off, in elementary school, the waste paper baskets were placed outside the bathroom itself. Oh, man!

I remember during recess everyone would be running around and playing tetherball or foursquare. I was cautious not to move around too much for fear the big pillow between my legs wouldn't stay in position. I wondered if anyone knew? No one seemed to be treating me differently. I wondered if anyone else had started menstruating? But when we watched the films about it in class, I could tell by the snickering that no one else had started. I just thought to myself, "You won't think it's so funny pretty soon. You'll see."

Is this what I had to look forward to? I thought becoming a mature woman was a good thing. What else was in store for me? I was already wearing a bra. Wasn't this the end? Well...

The Responsible One

I remember when my oldest sister got pregnant. I was about 12 or 13. Moma was so upset. I kept thinking, "What's the big deal? We have plenty of room in the house." Well, the big deal was girls that weren't married were not supposed to get pregnant. At least, unmarried "Arnold" girls weren't supposed to get pregnant. But here she was. The oldest daughter, in college, no husband, and pregnant.

I thought this was truly exciting. Her stomach got sooo big! Sometimes I could see the baby moving inside, and sometimes I would actually get to feel the baby moving. I used to wonder if all of that activity going on was healthy. I would ask my sister if it hurt, but she always laughed and said no. What was going on in there anyway? What was that baby doing? And when was it coming out? I wanted to see it. After all, I was going to be the loving aunt.

Well, when the baby finally came I was in seventh heaven. It was so little and cute. I wanted to hold the baby. I wanted to feed the baby. I wanted to bathe the baby. I would stay up all night listening for the baby. I was so afraid that the poor thing would need something, I couldn't sleep. Whenever I heard the slightest whimper, I was there. It didn't matter what time it was. I was the responsible one. I was going to take care of this baby if it was the last thing I did. Moma really got concerned because I was up all night. She kept telling me the baby would be okay and that I didn't have to worry. But how could I be sure? I would have died if something happened to that baby. The way I was acting, one would have thought it was MY baby!

You know it never even crossed my mind to ask about the baby's father. As far as I was concerned, he didn't exist. He wasn't there. My sister lived at home with us at the time. Maybe I was trying to make sure the baby didn't miss her father. I wanted her to know that whatever she needed, she would have. I would protect her. I would never leave her alone.

As she got older, she got cuter. She would make such funny faces and say such funny things. She called Moma "Nanny." It was Nanny this and Nanny that. She was Nanny's heart. She had captured everyone's heart.

We used to go to the park everyday. One time, I went across the street to the gym to watch the boys play basketball. I left the baby at the park playing. She was in no danger cuz' everybody knew who she was and would take care of her. I must have been gone for about 30 minutes. When I returned, she was crying her eyes out. She thought I'd left her. I felt so badly. I explained to her that I would never leave her. Didn't she know that? We stayed at the park extra long that day. By the time we got home, it was dark. Brother, this being responsible thing was much more than I had bargained for.

I used to cook her dinner all the time. Once, we had macaroni and cheese and hot dogs. Only I had forgotten to put the "cheese" in with the macaroni. Although she ate it and said it was good, I felt awful. So I put the cheese in, mixed it up real good, and asked her if she wanted some more. I told her she could even put catsup on it. Well, of course she went for that. And I felt vindicated.

I loved taking care of my niece. We did everything together. It was that experience that taught me the real meaning of responsibility. It was that experience that taught me having children was no game; it was serious business. It was that experience that made me know I'd never have children.

I felt as though I had grown up awfully fast. I felt very mature (and looked it too) and responsible. I didn't regret it. I've always looked forward to becoming a mature, sophisticated woman (like Nancy Wilson or Lena Horne). My motto was, "Bring it on cuz' I have things to do, people to see, and places to go!"

Conclusion

I remember at age 13 feeling like I had reached a significant milestone. I had become a young woman in spite of myself. I was wearing a bra, had already started my period, and had helped to care for an infant. I had witnessed abuse, experienced and understood every feeling from fear to ecstasy. I felt mature and very responsible. My childhood was over, and although I had no idea what was in store for me, I was ready to take it on.

Moma taught me to carry myself in a confident manner. She taught me not to take things or people for granted. She taught me the importance of friendship and treating my fellow man with respect and honor (even if I felt they didn't deserve it!).

I've always believed in God. As such, I also believe that there is a divine plan mapped out for each person. Each of us has a special *gift* with which we are to share. The challenge is to discover, accept, act, and be thankful for the many blessings that are bestowed upon us. I truly believe that my *gift* is one of writing. I've known since a very early age that one day I would write a novel. It's been a long time coming, but the reality is finally here.

It's not over; rather, it is just beginning. It's not been easy, but I wouldn't have it any other way. These short stories represent, to me, a journey through life. It has been exhilarating to reach back in my memory bank and document each incident. It has given me an opportunity to reflect on the people that have influenced my life. It has given me an opportunity to better understand myself and what's important to me. It has given me an opportunity to be less selfish and more appreciative of others.

Although I've changed the names of most of the people mentioned in these short stories (except for those of my family), I'm sure they know who they are. I am equally as sure of the surprise they will experience upon reading about themselves and the influence they have had on my life.

No one can ever really know the things children will remember or what may influence their lives the most. With this in mind, conduct yourself accordingly. Conduct yourself in a manner that you would want remembered. Give of yourself for you have so much to share.

To each and every person that has been a part of my life, I give a warm and heartfelt *thank you*. And I thank those of you, in advance, who will play a leading role in my next volume of memories.

God's richest blessings are yours. All that is required is belief and acceptance.

ABOUT THE AUTHOR

Vetress Arnold was born and raised in Yakima, Washington. She attended Whitworth College (Spokane, Washington), and graduated from the University of Washington (Seattle, Washington). She holds a Bachelor of Arts degree in English.

Vetress currently lives in Redondo Beach, California.

Printed in the United States
95377LV00004B/113/A